First Hard Ride

Sexy Stories Collection

VOLUME 11

10 EROTIC SHORT STORIES

KELLIE GRANIER

Publisher's Note: This is a work of fiction. Names,
characters, places, and incidents are a product of
the author's imagination. Locales and public
names are sometimes used for atmospheric
purposes. Any resemblance to actual people, living
or dead, or to businesses, companies, events,
institutions, or locales is completely coincidental.

First Hard Ride/ Kellie Granier. – 2nd ed.
Xplicit Press, an imprint of TLM Media LLC

ISBN-13: 978-1-62327-633-1
ISBN-10: 1-62327-633-0
eISBN: 978-1-62327-634-8

Printed in the United States of America

CONTENTS

1 HONEY'S REVIEW

Honey closed her eyes as the leather straps closed around her wrists. Steel cuffs closed over her ankles securing her to the spreader bar, hands and feet locked together, legs spread, shoulders back, pushing her tits higher in the air. Her long hair fell down her back in thick waves, and her scalp tingled with anticipation. Within seconds of locking the cuff, Dan buried his hand in her hair, gripping the tresses tightly, close to the skin. He yanked her head back, forcing her to meet his eyes as he stared down at her.

"Comfortable?"

"Yes, Dan," she quickly answered.

"Good. I wouldn't want my woman to be uncomfortable."

Honey licked her dry lips, ignoring the tightness in her buttocks. The position would be uncomfortable soon enough, but of course, there was no good reason to point that out. He massaged her scalp for a moment before clenching his fist again, and the sharp pain in her scalp quickly scattered through her body like sparks erupting. The heat between her legs grew, becoming more and more uncomfortable. He bent to rub his stubbed cheek against her jaw, letting his bristly hair scrape harshly across her tender skin, his fingers clenching again. Within seconds, the smell of her arousal was heavy in the air. She felt him smile against her warm cheek, and she wasn't sure if the flush in her face was embarrassment or excitement.

"I love how responsive you are. That's why you're Dan's best."

Honey's blush deepened at the deep words, and his sudden disappearance left her feeling chilled. She resisted the impulse to look over her shoulder to watch him--he didn't like her to be blindfolded but he also didn't approve of her keeping track of him. It was all she could do to stare at the floor, her heart hammering in her ears as she waited for his return. Every inch of her body strained towards him, her blood rushing from her head, her mind dizzy with possibilities. She didn't know if this was a punishment or a reward--though it wouldn't be long until that mystery was cleared up. Still, it was getting harder and harder to tell the two events apart. His punishments always felt so good and his rewards were always so maddening.

The soft leather of her favorite flogger tickled over her shoulders. He used the end to brush the hair away from her neck, exposing the tender skin between her shoulders to the deceptively soft leather. Goose bumps erupted down her spine and over her shoulders, the tiny hairs on the back of her neck standing on end. The leather tips danced over her skin, moving back and forth, spinning over her skin as he twirled his wrist. But then, the playful leather disappeared and when it came back, it was with a sharp sting. The sensation startled her and she tensed to brace for the next one, her pussy clenching as the sensation bled down her body to pool between her thighs.

He gathered her hair up in his left palm and pulled it off her back, holding it to the side while he brought the flogger down again and again with his right. Honey could imagine the welts erupting, the redness spreading, and then the bruises forming. But the pain quickly morphed into something else, and though she knew that each hard crack must have hurt, all she felt was heat; heat suffusing and surrounding her, wrapping her up into a tight cocoon.

The flogging stopped and she gasped for breath, her lungs allowed to operate once again. Her head fell forward as she struggled for the oxygen she so badly needed, but he didn't allow her the chance to rest. He yanked her head back again, and she blinked up at him, her lips parted, her chest rising and falling rapidly. She almost saw a smile in his eyes, though his face remained the same passive stone she'd come to expect from him. She almost returned the smile she thought she saw, but he struck fast, like a snake, claiming her mouth in a hard kiss. She automatically opened to him, allowing his tongue to sweep past her lips. Without breaking the kiss, he let the tips of flogger slide across the back of her shoulders, gently caressing her red and tender flesh.

She shuddered repeatedly under the gentle caress, her entire body shaking with the power of the oh-so-light sensation. Her pussy walls fluttered, and her outer lips were puffy and slick with desire. He might not touch her there at all--and if he did, it may not be for hours yet--but she was already desperate to feel his fingers sliding between her flesh and into her slit. She may have pumped her hips a few times, though she hoped he didn't notice that. If he knew there was something she wanted--or God forbid, something she needed--he would make it a point to deny her. How long that denial would last always varied, but Honey always found it to be much too long for her liking.

Just when the caresses reached the point of maddening, he switched back to the blows. Her fingers and toes curled as the dozens of leather straps that made the flogger's tail landed on her back. Her spine twisted and curved, her body jerking from one side to the other as he hit her until the sudden tight grip on her hair made her still.

"Don't try to get away from me. Don't ever pull away from me, Honey. I thought you liked it when I gave you special attention."

"I do, Dan."

"Then why are you trying to get away from me? Don't you know it hurts my feelings when he tries to do something nice for his woman and she's ungrateful?"

"I'm not ungrateful, Dan," Honey quickly protested. Stopping would be the worst outcome of all, and she didn't want that to happen.

"Then why do you keep pulling away?"

She swallowed. "I'm sorry."

"I didn't ask if you were sorry. I asked why you were doing it."

"The sting...it surprised me. I didn't mean to try to move away."

"So are you saying that I doesn't know how to flog his best woman?"

"No, no, Dan. Of course I wouldn't say that. It was just surprising. I won't try to pull away again, I promise."

"You better not. You better keep perfectly still. Do you understand me?"

"Yes, Dan," Honey whispered, imagining a steel rod holding her spine completely straight.

She curled her fingers into tight fists, hoping the sting of her nails would distract her from the much larger, much hotter sting of the flogger. The first blow on her left shoulder wasn't so bad, and for a few seconds, she thought she would be able to handle it. But her lover knew where all her most sensitive spots were, and it wasn't long until he found each one with the leather tails. The dull pressure of each blow would have been fine on its own, but he knew exactly how to snap his wrist to add an extra little sting at the end.

She lost track of the blows as they came

down, but she kept her spine straight and her shoulders locked. The slight tension in her buttocks and between her shoulders increased with each passing minute spent in the spreader bar, though it wasn't quite enough to distract her from the flogging. If anything, the discomfort heightened her awareness each time the flogger fell on her shoulders, lashed across her back and stung the thin skin along her ribs. By the time he tossed the flogger to the side, her muscles ached from the pressure of remaining completely still, tears flooded at the rims of her eyes, and her skin felt as tight as a drum.

"Did you like that?"

"Yes, Dan."

"You took that very well. I think you deserve a reward."

He moved to stand in front of her, and she watched with wide, greedy eyes as he unbuttoned his pants and pulled the fly down. He wasn't wearing underwear and so there was nothing to block her view of his thick, hard cock. She licked her lips with unconscious hunger, and it was a good thing for her that her hands were tied; otherwise she would be violating quite a number of rules and reaching for him. She loved Dan's cock, and often wished she had more of a chance to touch him, kiss him, smell him, and pleasure him the way she wanted to.

"Do you want my cock?"

"Yes, Dan," she breathed.

"Beg for it."

That wasn't hard to do. She was always on the verge of begging for it, and now it was so very, very close to her mouth. So close she really could smell his skin, and the intoxicating combination of his musk and pheromones left her sweating and trembling, her mouth watering for his smooth skin and the taste of him. Nobody else in the world tasted like Dan, and it was a delicacy she very rarely enjoyed.

"Please, Dan. Please let me suck your cock. I want to make you feel good, and I can Dan, please let me show you. Please let me give you that pleasure. Please let me try. Please."

He gripped the base of his cock and wiped the head across her mouth, leaving a trail of glistening pre-cum. She desperately wanted to lick the clear fluid away, but he didn't give her permission. She parted her lips, her tongue hovering just inside her lips, her mouth as wet for her dick as her pussy. He let the tip slide in, let it touch her tongue for what felt like a microsecond, and then pulled away again. She couldn't contain her moan, and she knew her frustration and hunger were stamped across her face. She couldn't keep anything from him anyway, but he must have been laughing at her at this point. She felt like she was starving for his cock, and starving people didn't exactly keep their tortured state a secret.

"Please," she whispered. "Please fuck my throat, Dan. Please, please."

This time, when the head slipped between her lips, it didn't immediately disappear. She dropped her jaw, turning her head slightly so she could swallow him to the base. As he filled her throat, blocking her air passages, she felt such a sense of satisfaction that it almost pushed her into an orgasm. Knowing she didn't have permission for that, she resisted the feeling, pushing back the rising wave of pleasure as she swallowed around his thick, throbbing shaft.

He used the hold he had on her hair to keep her head in place as he pulled back, or else she would have chased him with her mouth until she caught him again. He used that control to set a hard, pounding rhythm. Her throat bulged every time he thrust forward, and he kept himself buried in place at longer intervals, until he had her head smashed against his groin, her nose buried in his hair, her lips pulled tight around his thick base.

Her nostrils flared, and her chest heaved, but it didn't do any good. She couldn't get any air to her lungs. His cock seemed to grow thicker by the second, completely filling her mouth and throat, and her chest started to burn. Alarm bells went off in her mind, automatically triggered by the general lack of oxygen, but she ignored her body's warning. Her instincts told her to struggle, to fight against whatever was keeping her in place, whatever was suffocating her. But she ignored her instincts, too. She didn't need to give into her fear. That was one of the things he'd been teaching her, and now it seemed like she was getting the chance to put his lessons to practical use. Every time the alarmist inside of her shouted to twist away, the sub inside of her responded with cool logic: "He's not going to let any harm come to me."

She repeated that line again and again, her mantra, her lifeline. She managed to tilt her head just a half inch, but it was enough to allow the tiniest bit of air to flow through her nose. She inhaled desperately, her throat still clenching around his thick erection. He yanked free of her mouth without warning, taking long strands of spit and pre-cum with him as she choked and gasped for breath. Instead of enjoying her new oxygen, she immediately leaned forward, seeking out his dick again. She didn't know how long she'd have access to it, and she wanted it in her mouth no matter what. He chuckled lightly as she made a move for his cock, catching her hair and pulling her back just before her lips closed over him.

"Do you really want it?"

Honey nodded quickly. "Yes, yes, oh yes. Dan, please."

"Don't say I never gave you anything."

He wrapped her long hair once around his hand, bringing his fist to the base of her skull, and forced her head back. She opened her mouth again and he fed her his dick inch by inch, until his balls brushed against her chin. She'd been with many men before--and even had a few lovers before him--but nobody ever made her beg like this. Nobody else could give her so little and yet leave her so satisfied. He pumped his hips, moving his dick in and out of her mouth in a hard, almost frantic tempo. He fucked her throat with brutal intensity, and it wasn't long before the flesh at the back of her throat felt bruised and tender. Every time she swallowed after that, it would hurt, and she would think of him, and miss him, wet for him.

She heard him gasp, heard his breath catch in his throat, and readied herself for his load. But he didn't shoot down her throat. He pulled out at the last second, cupping his erection with his palm and giving himself one more stroke before catching the long strands of cum against his skin. She stared at his jerking shaft; her own body clenching each time pleasure wracked him, licking her lips hungrily.

"Do you think I'm going to let you taste my cum?" He chuckled darkly and brought his palm to his mouth, licking the white strings away. "Not yet, Honey. That's a privilege you have to earn."

"Yes, Dan."

"But you did a very good job." He relaxed his hold in her hair and caressed her cheek with his knuckles. She stared up at him, waiting, yearning, wishing every cell in her body wasn't already attuned to his. He considered her for a heavy moment and then bent to claim her mouth in another kiss. This one was far more gentle, his tongue a teasing, playful guest in her mouth rather than the force that literally stole her breath. She melted into the kiss, soft and pliant, so intoxicated by the unexpected tenderness that she didn't notice what his right hand was doing. Not until his fingers were buried between her lips, seeking out the hard pebble of her clit.

"Do you want to come, baby?" He asked without breaking the kiss.

"Yes, please, Dan. Please, may I?"

"You may. Right now."

Honey had never been good at controlling the timing of her orgasm, but he was training her with that, too. If she didn't come when he said she could, then she would be allowed to come at all for the rest of their play time. Maybe even the rest of the week. His words slithered through her, igniting a million fires under her skin that finally culminated in a bright white flash of bliss. She stiffened, her back arching, her feet pulling against the spreader bar, as her body gushed its pleasure all over Dan's fingers.

"Good," he murmured repeatedly as the aftershocks quaked through her body. He brought his slick fingers to his lips and licked them clean. "Very good. You're learning."

"Thank you, Dan," Honey said with a relaxed, blissful sigh. His praise meant more to her than the orgasm, and both left her warm and sated, slumped like melted wax. She wanted to lie down, but he made no move to release her from the spreader bar.

"But that was only the review. Catch your breath and then we'll get to the main lesson." With those words, he straightened and tucked his dick back into his pants. She couldn't do anything except watch him leave the room, chills soon replacing the shivers of pleasure, her frantic mind racing a mile a minute. With a million questions and no way to answer them, all she could do was waiting.

2 FRANK'S FIRST TIME

Frank nervously glanced at the computer clock for the twentieth time in as many minutes. Each group of sixty seconds went by far too slowly, but the minutes seemed to be racing by, bringing him ever close to five o'clock. Then he could make his escape for the weekend and put this week in the history books. He had mixed feelings about that--hadn't he been longing for a few days off from his far too demanding boss, Mr. Wheton? But now, that he was about to flee for his weekend, he couldn't deny the twinge of disappointment. He never exactly asked for Mr. Wheton's attention, but he never actually said "No!" either, and it was hard to say which he disliked more--receiving attention or being utterly ignored.

He tried to concentrate on the email he was drafting, but the words were blurring together and his fingers had declared themselves independent agents. He couldn't get an entire a down without fucking up at least two of the words, usually drastically changing the meaning of the sentence in the process. He was so distracted, he didn't even fully trust himself to edit the mess he was making and so, each sentence took twice as long as necessary to complete. At the rate he was going, he wouldn't have the email done by quitting time, which meant he wouldn't be able to leave at quitting time, which kept him in Mr. Wheton's sphere that much longer.

Frank's attention went to the silent phone, staring at it balefully. Why wasn't the light going off? Why wasn't it ringing? Mr. Wheton had been uncharacteristically silent all day. In fact, he'd been the ideal boss--leaving Frank alone to complete his mountain of tasks in peace. That was all Frank wanted, so he couldn't explain the unsettled feeling in his chest, the sense of waiting, of being pulled between Mr. Wheton's office and his own desk. He sat squarely in his chair, stared at his computer, and yet, his mind was behind that oak paneled door, and his thoughts swirled around Mr. Wheton.

When the intercom light flashed, Frank almost didn't believe it was real and not a product of his hopeful, yet wary, imagination. The light flashed again, and this time it was followed by the familiar snarl.

"Frank? Get your ass in here."

"Yes Mr. Wheton." Frank took a deep breath and gathered his notepad and pen. He wanted to bring his smartphone, too, but Mr. Wheton didn't like them for some reason. Or maybe he just didn't like knowing that Frank had a line to the outside world that he didn't even need his hands to use. He let himself into the older man's office, quickly and subtly searching his boss's face for any hint at his mood.

The signs weren't good. But, Frank assured himself, it wasn't anything he couldn't handle. He'd seen the boss in worst moods, and besides, if anybody was prepared to deal with his moods, it was Frank. That was why he'd been the Big Man's secretary for the past year--so far that was six months longer than anybody else managed.

"How can I help you, sir?"

"Get over here." He gestured Frank over to the desk and pointed at the letter sitting in the middle of the blotter. "What is this?"

"It looks like an invoice."

"Yes. An invoice to Mr. Jeremy"

"Is it not correct, sir?"

"No, it's not. I wasn't going to charge him for the last meeting, and now he's received this bill? What's he going to think of me? What's he going to think of my staff? We're going to have to fix this."

"Yes sir. I'll get it taken care of ASAP."

"I shouldn't have to put up with crap like this," he bit out. "You know your job. Why do I have to tell you your business when I have my own to attend to?"

"It won't happen again, Mr. Wheton."

Frank decided it was wise not to point out that he never informed his secretary of the deal he struck with Mr. Jeremy. Frank was very talented, and he could manage Mr. Wheton's career and life better than anybody else, but he wasn't quite a psychic. Still, this was simple enough to rectify, and if it was all the highly respected lawyer had to complain about, Frank would consider this a good week.

"See, that it doesn't. Now get over here." He patted his lap, making it perfectly clear where he wanted Frank to be. "Are you wearing your new present? Let me see it."

Frank answered by unbuckling and unbuttoning his pants, pushing them down his thighs to reveal the pink, lacy thong he'd been wearing all day. It was a little uncomfortable, but fit him surprising well. And he'd never admit it out loud, but he liked the way it held his junk. The tightness around his balls had been driving him crazy all day. He'd made it a point to wear them every day that week, washing them in the sink when he got home at night and stepping out of the shower and into them the next morning.

"Leave your pants off."

He did, kicking the garment away with his loafers. From the waist up, he looked like a professional assistant of a very important lawyer. From the waist down, he was nothing but a dirty slut, that same lawyer's little slut. He sat on Mr. Wheton's lap, his cock half-hard as soon as he settled on the man's crotch. Mr. Wheton's dick was hard, too, jutting against Frank's tightly covered ass. Mr. Wheton's hand immediately went to Frank's cock, and he gripped it with strong fingers. Frank swallowed down his gasp as Mr. Wheton gave him a good squeeze, molding his palm against the bulge in the mink material. His long fingers moved lower to cup his balls, and the pain from that hold brought black dots to Frank's vision.

"Do you like your present?"

"Very much so, sir."

"Are you going to wear these for me every day?"

"Yes, sir."

"Good boy. I wish I didn't have to punish you today." He squeezed Frank's balls again. "When are you ever going to learn?"

"I won't make this mistake again, sir."

"Sure, that's what you say." Mr. Wheton moved quickly, lifting Frank from his lap and pinning him face down to the desk, holding him with one hand on his neck and the other at the small of his back. Frank's ass stuck up in the air, completely exposed, nothing guarding against the harsh slap of his boss's large hand. He did it a second time with enough force to make the blow crack like a gun shot, and red-hot pain rushed up from Frank's cheek. He squeezed his eyes shut, face screwing up as a blow of equal intensity fell on his other cheek. "But how do I know you're telling the truth?"

"I didn't lied to you, sir," Frank gasped out, more than a little offended.

"I know you don't, boy. But, that doesn't mean you're telling the truth, either." He massaged Frank's ass with both hands, working the pain out of the flesh, coaxing Frank into relaxing. He gripped the edge of the desk, his cheek pressed to the blotter, his erection smashed between his body and the unforgiving wood. Before too long, that promised to be far more uncomfortable than any of Mr. Wheton's slaps.

"But, you're going to have the chance to prove yourself to me."

"How, sir?" Frank couldn't keep the

eager note from his voice. Sometimes he hated the old bastard, and sometimes he resented his position, but he couldn't ever stand up for himself. Because at the end of the day, he wanted a chance to prove himself, wanted a chance to please and earn Mr. Wheton's gratification. The few times he'd earned praise from the old goat had been the most satisfying times of his life--and he meant satisfying on every level, including sexual.

"I'm having a small get together for some of my closer, like-minded friends. As my personal assistant, I expect your participation in this event."

"Yes, of course sir. What do you want me to do?" He expected he'd be sending invitations, hiring caterers, and taking over all the little details Mr. Wheton never thought of, much less cared about. And maybe he would be doing that, too, but that's not the answer he got.

"I want you to service every single one of them. No matter what they ask for, how they ask for it, and where they ask for it. Your job is to please them like you please me, because, that will please me. Do you think you're up to it?"

Frank was not in the position to give a negative answer--literally. With his head down and his ass in the air--encased in pink silk--it really didn't seem like he could give any answer but "Yes, sir."

"Good boy. Don't worry. The guest list is very...elite. I wouldn't waste you on somebody who couldn't appreciate your talents." With that, he peeled the silk from Frank's body, slowly revealing his rounded ass before dragging the material down his legs. Frank caught his breath as the silk slid against his skin, caressing and taunting him. It was such a heady contrast to the pain of Mr. Wheton's palm falling on his flesh that he moaned-- exactly like the dirty little slut Mr. Wheton pegged him as the first day of his employment.

Mr. Wheton's fingers were smooth; his skin pampered and well cared for, his nails filed down to smooth crescents. He dragged his fingers up and down Frank's ass, the tips sliding into the crack to tease the sensitive nerves there. Frank bit his lip and held himself from shifting back, more blood rushing to his trapped dick. He tried to look over his shoulder to see Mr. Wheton's face, to try to read his intentions, but the hand on the back of his head kept him from moving. He had no choice but to stare at the wall as Mr. Wheton continued the slow, sensual exploration.

"Have you had anything in your ass this week?" Mr. Wheton asked conversationally.

"No, sir."

"Have you jacked off this week?"

"No, sir." He never received permission from Mr. Wheton for either of those activities, which meant he had to take a handful of melatonin pills to fall asleep every night, since he couldn't just rub one out and then pass out.

"Good boy," Mr. Wheton sighed, his finger suddenly probing Frank's sphincter. Frank took a deep breath just as the fingertip breached the tight muscle. Mr. Wheton slid his dry finger deep into Frank's ass, seemingly unmindful of the level of Frank's discomfort. It would have felt better with lube--still, it didn't exactly feel bad. Frank pulled his bottom lip between his teeth and resisted the urge to push back. He heard Mr. Wheton's breath come faster and faster as he pumped his wrist, twisting his finger with every push forward.

He added a second finger without warning, and Frank nearly choked on his moan. The pain flared up, but as before, it faded beneath the growing pleasure. Before Frank came to work for Mr. Wheton, he never had a single thing in his ass; fact that seemed to positively delight the old dragon. He periodically gave Frank instructions to insert various objects into his ass, but this was the first time he'd taken matters into his own hands. It was the first time anybody had fingered Frank, and he just wasn't quite sure what to think of it--except that a large part of him liked it rather a lot.

"I know you're nervous," Mr. Wheton continued. "I was nervous my first time, too. But it's okay. I'll take good care of you."

Frank heard the left bottom drawer slide open and closed and then the fingers disappeared. When they returned, they were slick and cold with some lubricant-- maybe lotion. Frank sighed with pure pleasure as the slick fingers slid inside of him--this time there was no raw burning, just the satisfaction of sensitive skin and tender flesh finally being touched. He keened and wiggled backwards, eagerly encouraging Mr. Wheton to thrust even deeper inside of him.

"They're going to fuck you. And I'm going to want to watch. In all my years, young Frank, I never found a boy I want to see spoiled as much as you."

Frank wasn't sure if he should take that as a compliment, or if he should be disturbed and scared. He didn't think he should be achingly hard, but he was, and his balls were throbbing in rapid time with his heart. Was Mr. Wheton going to fuck him? Is this where there weird game had been heading the entire time? Well, of course he was--and of course this was his goal all along. Frank recognized that, but still he was somehow surprised.

The pink panties were suddenly in front of his face. Mr. Wheton pulled his head up by the back of his hair and shoved the panties into his mouth. Frank automatically tried to spit them out, but Mr. Wheton just pushed them even deeper and held his palm over Frank's mouth, sealing it shut.

"Trust me; you'll be thankful in a few seconds. Can't have security rushing in because they've heard strange sounds, now can we?"

Frank nodded his understanding, tasting his own stink on the silk layered over his tongue. The lubed fingers returned to ass, a third one carefully added. He worked the three digits deeper, spreading the lube and opening Frank up, stretching him to accommodate Mr. Wheton's much thicker cock. Frank had seen it more than once and knew it was going to feel far, far different from the fingers sliding in and out of him. He probably couldn't take the thick flesh without screaming, and he definitely didn't want anybody rushing into the office to see him in this position.

"I know you've never been fucked before, but don't worry. It'll only hurt for a little bit. Are you scared?"

Frank shook his head. No, he wasn't scared of Mr. Wheton--not anymore at any rate. He'd been terrified of Mr. Wheton when he pulled him from the secretarial pool, and positively petrified the first time he called Frank into his office and made it clear what his interests were. But now, Mr. Wheton didn't scare him--or if he did, that fear was tempered considerably by his own dark desires. Now there wasn't anything Mr. Wheton wanted that some part of him didn't want as well. Even now, he had no desire to fight for his freedom, even though he was about to be penetrated.

Mr. Wheton's dick pressed against his lubed muscle, the firm head pushing forward harder and harder, against the automatic resistance of Frank's body. Frank bit down around the panties, trying to swallow his scream as the pain sliced through him. He was being split in two, torn apart, and his flesh burned in response. He squeezed his eyes shut, breathing heavily through his nose as Mr. Wheton worked to claim every inch of him. It felt like an eternity passed before the older man pressed up against him, his balls fitting snugly against Frank's taint.

"Oh, you're tight boy. Goddamn...goddamn...you're so tight..."

Frank whimpered his face hot and damp with sweat and tears. He stretched his arms, gripping the desk above his head and holding on tight as Mr. Wheton slid out and then slammed forward again, reclaiming those precious inches he lost. The man's hands went to Frank's hips, his fingers sinking into the firm flesh there, holding him firmly in place while he pumped his hips. The desk rattled with each thrust, moving across the hard-wood floor in tiny but unmistakable increments. Frank rocked back partially to meet the thrusts, partially to relieve the pressure on his groin.

He never expected the reach-around from Mr. Wheton, but he was so grateful when he felt the long fingers close around his dick that his knees went out. He willed the strength back to his legs, pushing up from the desk just enough to rock back and then thrust forward into Mr. Wheton's dry, smooth hand. At first, Frank didn't quite know how to move, didn't know how fast to go or how to meet Mr. Wheton's rhythm, but then he found the primal beat he needed to follow. He spit and spluttered, forcing the panties from his mouth as he fucked himself on Mr. Wheton's dick and fucked his cock into Mr. Wheton's fist.

"Come, boy. I know you want to. Let me feel it."

Frank didn't want to come just yet. He liked the long tendrils of pleasure climbing up his spine and the sparks exploding behind his eyes and raining down his body. He liked the powerful thrusts, the sense of being overwhelmed and overpowered even as he gave in to desires he couldn't even acknowledge before. But he wasn't in the habit of ignoring Mr. Wheton, either, and so he focused on the pleasure, focused on the waves growing higher and higher, crashing harder and harder through his frame.

He bucked up, his spine locking, his hips going crazy as his balls pulled tighter. Mr. Wheton squeezed and pulled, coaxing him closer and closer to his release. With nothing stopping him and a week's worth of blue balls behind him, it was all too easy to let go and erupt into Mr. Wheton's hand. While he rocked his hips with the aftershocks, he felt Mr. Wheton tensing behind him. But he pulled out before he burst, shooting his load onto Frank's ass. He felt the warm liquid drip down his skin, coating his cheeks and the back of his thighs.

"Go clean yourself up. We have a party to plan."

"Yes, sir," Frank muttered as he straightened. He found he couldn't quite look Mr. Wheton in the eye as he hurried to the private bathroom--and he couldn't quite keep the smile from his face as he studied himself in the mirror.

3 THE NUN GAME

Kitty and Honey don't question their Master, and when they come home to find two nun's habits waiting for them, they quickly change. Kitty is excited about the new game, but Honey is trepidatious, even uncomfortable. But she trusts her Master, and she only wants to please him, so she sets her discomfort aside. When they descend to the basement, Honey quickly falls into the role of Sister Mary, but how far will this playacting take her?

Kitty and Honey found the clothes laid out with a note instructing them to dress and join Sir in the basement. It was signed, rather mysteriously, by 'The Priest' and a quick inspection of the clothes revealed they were nun habits. Kitty thought it was all very funny, but Honey wasn't far removed from the Catholic education of her youth, and for the first time she felt uncomfortable with something Sir asked her to do. It wasn't enough to make her refuse him, thus earning serious punishment, but she was the mirror contrast to Kitty's bubbly excitement as they descended to the basement.

Sir waited for them in the basement, which had been rearranged to look more like an austere dorm room than a BDSM dungeon, his tall figure even more imposing in a traditional kassok. Honey's stomach fluttered at the sight of him, and she felt smaller somehow – or maybe he was taller. He smiled down at them, making eye contact with each one before greeting in a silky smooth voice, "Good evening Sister Catherine, Sister Mary. I'm Antonio, and I'm so happy you could join me tonight. Please have a seat."

Honey was Sister Mary now and with that designation she felt herself sinking away, allowing a new personality to rise to the surface. Sister Mary was new to the order, had only just taken her orders, and she was more than a little intimidated by Antonio. He was the most powerful man she knew, and one of the very few men she came into regular contact with. He made her feel like a young woman, not a grown woman who chose to commit herself to Christ. With a sidelong glance, Honey saw that Kitty was sinking into character as well. The silly smile was gone, and though she still buzzed with a certain energy, her eyes were downcast, demur. They both shuffled over to the newly set up cot and perched on the edge as instructed.

"I was so proud last Sunday when you two took your orders to fully join our convent. You are both so spiritual, I can feel Christ's love when I look at you." He smiled kindly. "But there's one more thing you have to do in order to complete the process."

Sister Mary frowned, confused. "What do you mean? Mother Superior never mentioned that."

"That's because it's not her place to have this conversation. In fact, we mustn't discuss this outside of this room. If I hear you mention one word of it to anybody, I will be forced to punish you. I won't want to, but that's how serious this matter is. Do you understand?"

"Yes," they both murmured.

"Good, good. Now, you are both brides of Christ, meaning you're spiritually bonded to our Lord and Savior. But every bridegroom must have his wedding night."

"But...we're not allowed to know pleasures of the flesh."

"Yes, but that only applies to flesh and

blood men."

"Then how will there be a wedding night?"

Antonio's smile shifted and he gently cupped the back of Sister Mary's head. "Through me, my child. I've prayed a long time over this, and I've been chosen to be Christ's vessel. He will know you both through me."

"H-how can that be?"

"It's one of God's mysteries." He brushed his thumb over Sister Mary's lips. "Are you afraid? You needn't be. I promise, no harm will come to you. It's a very natural and beautiful thing."

"But...won't that make me a whore?" Sister Mary whispered.

"How could a bride welcoming her bridegroom into her bed be considered a whore? No, you've been chosen as well. Not everybody here is allowed to experience such...joy."

"Is that why we shouldn't say anything?" Sister Catherine asked.

He cupped her face with his free hand, looking down at both of them with a paternal smile of affection. "Precisely. We wouldn't want your sisters to be jealous because they weren't chosen. How do you think that would make them feel?"

"What should we do?" Sister Mary asked.

"First, it's important to prepare the

vessel for Christ's arrival. Come here, kneel as though you were taking communion."

The two young nuns were quick to obey his command, positioning themselves at his feet, their faces upturned in anticipation of further instruction. He pushed his hand through the folds of his kossak and then pulled his manhood from the robe. It was still limp, and though Honey had seen his dick many times, Sister Mary still reacted like a sheltered virgin, her ears turning a bright red as her gaze darted away.

"Now don't be shy. It's just another part of my body, no different from an arm or a leg. Does the sight of my arm make you uncomfortable, Sister Catherine?"

"No."

"And you, Sister Mary? Are you embarrassed by a toe?"

"No, I'm not."

"Then don't be shy now. As I said, I need your help preparing for my role. Stick out your tongue Sister Mary. Good. Now..." He gripped the base of his cock and touched it to Sister Mary's tongue. She tried to flinch away from the contact, but his other hand held her head in place. She was so deep in the role that the taste of his skin felt foreign, alien, even upsetting. She tried to turn her head away, but his grip was like a steel vice, and she was forced to hold her mouth open for his member.

"Lick me, my child."

She obeyed, flicking her tongue over his head.

"Have you ever had an ice cream cone, sweetheart?" His voice was low and patient, soothing. "Lick me like that."

With his words echoing in her head, she had no choice but to do as he instructed. She dragged her tongue around his crown until she felt his flesh start to move. It twitched against her tongue and she jerked away in surprise, her attention flying to his face.

"That's what it's meant to do," he said encouragingly. "That's how we know your bridegroom will be here soon. Here, give Sister Catherine a chance."

Sister Mary sat back and watched with a surprising twinge of jealousy as Sister Catherine accepted his manhood. After watching Sister Mary, she didn't need any further instruction from him. He closed his eyes and sighed. "That's it. He's going to be here any minute now. You need to be ready for him."

"How can I prepare for him?"

"A bride wouldn't meet her bridegroom with so many clothes on. Stand up here and undress."

Sister Mary blushed again, but again didn't hesitate to obey. It took her longer to undress than it did to dress, her limbs made heavy by shyness and a sense of guilt, like she was doing something wrong. By the time she was fully nude, her skin felt like it was a permanent shade of red, and his manhood had grown another two inches.

"Beautiful," he breathed. "Oh, Sister Mary, you're so spiritual. I can feel Heaven's power surging inside of me. Come here, it's your turn again."

As she sank to her knees, Sister Catherine rose to disrobe. Antonio's cock had been soft, almost spongey before, but now he was solid as a rock in her mouth. She couldn't resist running her tongue up and down his length, curious about the strange change in texture, size, even taste. A voice in the back of her mind worried that they might actually be doing the devil's bidding, but Antonio was so wise, so powerful, so...Godly. It seemed impossible that Lucifer might have corrupted his soul.

"Now that I'm ready, we need to make sure both of you are prepared for Christ's power. It can be very overwhelming, but I know of a way to help with the pain."

"It hurts?"

"For some. But as I said, I know of a way to mitigate that. Sister Mary, I want you to lay on the bed." He helped her to her feet and guided her to the cot. She lay back, her arms crossed over her chest, her knees touching. Antonio gently pulled them apart, pushing her legs wider and wider until she knew there was nothing protecting her most secret place. "Sister Catherine, join her, please. Yes, right here between her legs." He used his thumb and forefinger to spread her lips, and she felt a flood of shame as he stared down at her.

"She looks very pretty doesn't she, Sister Catherine? She reminds me of a flower. A beautiful, dewy rose. Roses are among God's most beautiful creations, don't you think?"

"Yes."

"Lick her pretty little rose, Sister Catherine. Go on, it's fine. You'll like it. You know how soft rose petals are? She's softer."

Sister Catherine ducked her head and her tongue fluttered over Sister Mary's flesh. She jerked as her sister touched her, her thighs quivering. A light touch on her hip kept her still as Sister Catherine's tongue found her skin again...and again...and again. Soon, the shock was gone and it only felt good. Very, very good. She closed her eyes and whimpered slightly, her thighs unconsciously opening further, her body rising from the cot in tense anticipation. Sister Catherine's shyness fell away and she attacked Sister Mary with a greedy tongue, lapping at her skin hungrily. She was getting slicker by the second and she knew that just wasn't from Sister Catherine's mouth.

"That's it," Antonio encouraged. "You're doing such a good job. Lick her lower. Do you taste that? Mmm, it's sweet, isn't it? That's what it tastes like when a bride is ready for her husband. Isn't that right, Sister Mary?"

"Wh-what?"

"Do you feel as though you're ready for your bridegroom?"

She felt all hot and sticky, frustrated and aching in a way she couldn't describe. It reached deep into body, and for the first time, she was aware of those depths. Aware of a part of her body she'd never wanted to think about before. She understood on a basic level that she needed to be filled, and now his rock-hard manhood made sense.

"Y-yes."

"Excellent. Move aside, please, Sister Catherine."

The loss of her mouth was like a physical pain, and she automatically reached for the other woman, but Antonio blocked her, taking Sister Catherine's place between her legs. He gripped her by the back of her knees and forced her legs wide open, wider than ever before. He'd removed his robes at some point and he loomed above her with dark skin and even darker body hair. His manhood jutted in front of him, his balls hanging low between his thighs. He slid his member up and down her lips, slicking himself with her arousal and Sister Catherine's spit.

Then she felt his head nudge her slit and her stomach fluttered. She swallowed, trying to wet her suddenly parched throat, but that didn't help. She opened her mouth, as if to say something, but before she could say a word, he was inside of her. She gasped, her legs folding around him as she took him to the hilt.

"That's it, Sister Mary. Can you feel Christ's love?"

"I...I don't know."

"Just relax. Let it happen. And it will happen, my child. It will."

Sister Mary nodded, or tried to nod. It was difficult to respond at all, difficult to think, and she never felt anything like this. She didn't try to follow what he did, didn't try to control her movements at all. Her mind was completely detached from her body, and her body only knew how to follow his rhythm. She rocked and vibrated with each powerful thrust, pain and pleasure mingling and spreading from her throat to her toes. The cot creaked beneath them, each ominous sound buried under her moans and his harsh, loud grunts.

He picked up speed, plowing faster and

faster into her welcoming body. The tension built inside of her, heat flaring through her veins, and she felt her muscles tighten as she rushed closer to her edge.

"Are you ready for it now? Are you ready to feel Him?"

"Yes...please...please...yes...."

Antonio reached between them, his long fingers finding her pulsing nub. She jerked her hips at the contact, a howl erupting from her throat. The pleasure was the complete opposite of everything she felt before, the complete fulfillment of the emptiness, the satisfaction of her hunger. She arched her back, pulling taut and writhing back and forth with the force of her bliss. She might have screamed—might have slipped and used his actual name—but everything was a complete blur.

And then it was over, and he pulled his half-soft manhood from her, leaving her satisfied and aching in a good way. She could do nothing but watch as he stood and walked over to Sister Catherine. He looped one arm around her waist and bent her over, holding her there as he thrust into her. She cried out, bracing her hands on her knees, but she was so much smaller than him, so much weaker, that it wasn't hard for him to keep her in place.

He drilled into her with as much force

as he used on Sister Mary, maybe more. Somehow, she felt every single thrust echoing in her own body, as though he shared his energy with both of them. Watching his hips piston in and out of her, watching his powerful body flex, while she absorbed each of the blows, made Sister Mary wet again, made her nub harden and stand at attention. Her hand moved to the wet triangle between her thighs, and Antonio's sharp eyes didn't miss the gesture.

"Did you like that? You want to feel it again, don't you? Well go ahead. Touch yourself. Play with your pussy while you watch me fuck her. Do you wish it was you, hmm? Do you want to feel me inside of you again?"

She caressed herself with each word, moving her fingers faster and faster as he spoke. The syllables were almost lost in grunts and gasps for air, but the deep timbre of his voice wrapped around her, pulling tight on her limbs and her spine, holding her as effectively as any chains. Sister Catherine moaned louder and louder, the sounds of her pleasure almost inhuman, but undeniably sexy.

"Let me watch you come, my child," Antonio urged. "Welcome His love inside of you once again."

His words sparked something inside of her—a short fuse on the end of a thousand fireworks. She went off, screaming and pumping her hips wildly, her fingers working furiously over her clit, pinching and squeezing and rubbing with just enough pressure to keep the fire burning. It felt so good, she almost really believed it was the light of God's love filling her. She could tell from their sounds that they weren't far behind, and Sister Catherine keened her satisfaction in between sobs for more.

Antonio walked Sister Catherine over to the cot, and as soon as the other woman collapsed on top of her, the spell was broken. She wasn't a nun, she was just Honey, and the woman she held in her trembling arms was her best friend and fellow slave, Kitty. And the man watching them with a small smile of pure satisfaction wasn't a priest, but he was the leader of their little flock and she was full of gratitude and love for him.

She definitely hoped they played this game again.

4 UNDER THE MASK

Candee has control issues, and they are beginning to harm her sexual adventures and relationships. So there's only one thing to do: push herself past her limits. After months of conditioning herself for full sensory deprivation, she dons a gas mask. and invites her favorite playmates to have their wicked way with her.

Candee had a pretty good sense of time. She was almost always right when she guessed at the time if a clock wasn't available. She didn't even need an alarm clock to wake up in the morning, even when her schedule was hectic and she didn't keep regular sleeping hours. But she completely lost any sense of the passage of time with the gas mask over her head. She couldn't see through the blackened eye covers, she couldn't hear through the thick material, and she had no idea what was happening around her. Five seconds passed only slightly quicker than five minutes, and those five minutes could easily stretch into an eternity.

A hand on her shoulder forced her down to her knees. She settled in the proper position, with her hands behind her back, her chest forward, her head lowered. Once the hand disappeared, she couldn't get any sense of where the man went, how many others were there with him, or what they were doing. The thick carpet cushioned her knees and completely muffled the sound of approaching footsteps, and she knew her playmates well enough to know none of them would utter a word. They'd maintain perfect silence, using familiar gestures and sign language to communicate with each other while they took her apart, bit by bit.

Candee once hated sensory deprivation. The first time she played with the gas mask, it completely set her off and brought the entire scene to a standstill. The combination of being bound and completely ignorant to everything around her was too much to accept, and she automatically plunged into full fight or flight mode. She could have left it at that--

nobody was making her wear the mask, and she didn't have to play with sensory deprivation if she didn't like it. But she'd been disappointed in herself--more than disappointed. She wasn't going to let a childish fear defeat her, nor was she going to succumb to her need for complete control.

She started wearing the gas mask on her own time, when she was going about her daily chores. She cleaned the house, cooked dinner, played her Xbox 360, and basically lived in mask with full visibility and nearly complete aural clarity until she was accustomed to the pressure and feeling of the headgear. Then it was time to start working on her senses.

Now three months after that first disastrous attempt, she was sitting in the middle of the same circle, only this time she had a much better idea of what to expect and how to deal with her responses. Around her stood a half dozen of her favorite playmates, each of them armed with their own favorite toy. Candee didn't know what they selected--blades, leather, candles, fire, feathers, spikes, ice, it could have been anything. She wouldn't know until it touched her, and when it did, she wouldn't be able to anticipate or control her reaction. She was already trembling with anticipation, and struggling to keep her imagination from running away with her. She couldn't predict what was going to happen to her, and respecting that fact went a long way to easing her control issues.

Somebody grabbed her by the arms roughly and yanked them behind her back, holding her hands together and wrapping a soft nylon rope around her wrists. She wiggled her fingers as layer after layer wrapped around her, pulling tighter and tighter. A moment later, the same was being done to her feet, and the two ropes were then tied together, pulling her arms tight and locking them in place. It was merely uncomfortable at the moment, but she knew her shoulders would soon start burning.

A fine, cool mist sprayed over her chest, and the chill immediately settled into her flesh. The mist continued over her arms and back and breasts and even the soles of her feet. The initial chill felt good, but as it covered her whole body, she began to shiver, goose bumps exploding down her spine and across her thighs. And then without warning, the sensation shifted, a hot flush instantly replacing the bone-deep chill. She was covered in it?perhaps an entire spray bottle of Icy-Hot slicked her body.

The spray infused her, until she was both cold and hot, flushed and shivering through every long second. Two large hands cupped her breasts, kneading the tender flesh with strong fingers until her nipples started to harden. He?for the hands undoubtedly belonged to male?tweaked each nipple, twisting the hard nubs until pain flared through her chest. She gasped into the mask, a soundless, unknown reaction as the pain increased, filling her whole world and blocking out any other sensation. When the pressure suddenly disappeared, she whimpered with gratitude, her breath coming in quick gasps as she tried to process and work through the inflicted agony.

But cold steel clamps replaced the fingers, closing over the now bruised and throbbing flesh. There was no getting away from this pain, no pulling away from the clamps, no escaping. Gradually, she became aware of the flush from the Icy Hot, and the two sensations somehow managed to coexist with the sharp edge of cold slicing through her torso. And that was the moment the clips were struck, slapped off her tender flesh. She screamed, the sound echoing in her mask, bouncing back into her ears. Her tits throbbed, and her eyes tingled with tight tears as the clamps were replaced and secured once again. She wasn't aware of the chain hanging between them until she felt a sharp tug on both nipples. The chain was then attached to the collar around her neck.

Her heart hammered in her ears and the sound of her breathing filled the mask. She recognized the warning tendrils of her anxiety as questions filled her mind. What was coming next? Was this all going to be breast torture and bondage? Should she have specified not to focus in any one spot? Each one reflected an aspect she longed to control, but she wasn't going to use the gesture they'd agreed on for her safe word. She wasn't. She was going to see this through, going to push through the stress and pain to find the pleasure of submission and release.

A knife's dull, cool edge scraped over her shoulder and down her ribs, traveling over the contours of her body. She could tell it was large?probably at least six inches and she imagined Percy wielding it with casual confidence. His blade was an extension of his body, and nobody had any question that he was a master. An artist. Just the thought of Percy standing over her was enough to make her shiver with pleasure. The blade turned and the sharp tip glided across the small of her back before pressing into the dimple of her hip.

From there, it was impossible to track the journey as the tip roamed over her body, the pressure gradually increasing until it broke the dermis, leaving a long, thin scratch down her shoulder. She felt a single drop of blood form and then slide down the length of her arm. It was hot and slow, faint and ticklish and she would have wiped it away if she could. The knife traveled along her arm again, pressing the mark ever deeper, coaxing up more tiny drops of heat to sear her flesh. It was all she could do to stop herself from leaning into the blade. She remained perfectly still, but the pain of the blade and the edge of a knife always called to her. There was nothing unpleasant about that sensation, nothing she didn't love.

Her breath was hot and fast, caught up in the mask and cycling through her lungs. A sudden rush of hot smoke overwhelmed her, and she realized somebody had a joint at the end of the tube. As soon as she inhaled, the room started to spin. She dropped down a little, eyes falling shut and the darkness behind her lids matched the darkness in the mask. The herbal smell of the weed invaded her nose and clung to her skin, layering over the blackness and the nuanced pain of the blade. Her head was spinning, and she felt like she was drowning with a lungful of burning air.

The blade disappeared, and the tickle softness of a feather took its place. She giggled and shivered, and once she started giggling, she couldn't stop. Her shoulders shook and her muscles trembled and the giggles grew to bigger and bigger guffaws. More and more feathers were added to the assault, and she couldn't bend or twist away from them. She couldn't stop laughing, and the sound built on itself, growing louder and louder, and the tickling inched closer to torture. Feather tips traced over her nipples, skittered along her ribs, and then scuttled over a most sensitive point in the small of her back. Goose bumps blanketed her, every inch of bare skin puckered as the chills tripped through her.

She felt the soft tickle of something new?leather rather than feathers. She automatically tensed in anticipation, knowing that she wouldn't be feeling the soft caress of suede for very long?soon it would sting. And sting it did when a sharp flick of a wrist brought the flogger down on her back. It fell again on the next breath, though this time there was no sting. Just a dull, heavy thud sending vibrations all through her flesh. There were still feathers dancing all over her, and the give and take of the contrasting sensations merged into one rolling wave of pleasure, covering every inch of her, even the bits that had yet to be touched.

The flogger started to land in a regular rhythm, raining down on her shoulders and back. It didn't hurt. There was no sting. Just a solid, steady thump that reverberated through her entire body. Soon, her breathing was pulled into the rhythm, and her heart rate slowed. Marijuana smoke filled her mask once again and she took a deep breath before floating away, carried by the steady thwack-thwack-thwack of the flogger.

Rough fingers pulling on her clit yanked her back to Earth, her hips suddenly jerking and twitching on their own volition. Her clit throbbed, becoming swollen and hard beneath the attention. She bit her lip and whimpered, grinding down on the fingers, her pussy slick with arousal, the juices slicking her thighs as well. The hard, cool head of a dildo replaced the fingers on her clit, grinding hard into her tender flesh. She rose up, shifted her hips, tried to coax the rubber dick into her throbbing pussy. Her fingers twitched, her spine arched, but the dick remained against her clit. The pleasure built and doubled and built on itself some more, and she was going to ignite...she was so close...

And then it all disappeared. The sudden lack of any sensation whatsoever was almost a physical pain, and she felt like she'd been dropped from a great distance to land flat on her chest. Her breath felt like it had been knocked out of her lungs, and the disappointment left her feeling hollow and wanting. She waited and waited, wondering if they were still surrounding her, or if they had left her to suffer for an interminable length of time. Her heart beat out each lonely, aching second, but no amount of time could cool the blood in her veins or bring her back down from her endorphin rush.

Time slowed, crawled, weighed down her limbs, and scraped over her skin and her hair. Her shoulders began to burn, her leg muscles tensed, and no amount of rocking or fidgeting could relieve the tension under her skin. It mounted and mounted, and she wondered if they could hear her pleas, her moans, her sighs, if they knew how much she needed from them, how much she wanted. More. More than this endless waiting. She imagined they must have left the room, must have snuck away to giggle and laugh at her torment. Or maybe they were all standing directly above her, looming and smirking, prepared to find more delicious ways to drive her insane.

The touch, when it came, was like a ray of sun after a long, cold winter. Fingernails across the back of her neck, not as sharp as the knife, but still sharp enough to sting. A hand cupping her pussy, fingertips pushing between her swollen labia to find her aching clit once again. The touches were so light, almost nothing at all, but her entire frame began to shake. She trembled more and more intensely, her entire body quaking, and heat pooled between her legs. Her breath hitched, caught in her throat by another cloud of smoke, and then she was soaring. Soaring higher than she ever thought possible. The pleasure wasn't tied to any one thing, the orgasm not anchored to earth, or even to any sense of reality. She was boundless, flying well beyond the constraints of the mask, of the rope, even of her own body. She lost track of everything, she didn't know what was real or in her own mind, who was touching her or where, how much was even real and what was merely memory.

Strong arms closed around her shoulders, pulling her back against a solid chest. A vibrator touched her pussy, and her pussy convulsed, clenching and releasing rapidly. The vibe felt like an electric circuit sending sparks sizzling under her skin, up and down her spine, tipping her into another cycle of pleasure, of higher and higher peaks. And when it was time to fall again, when she couldn't stop her watery muscles from collapsing, the arms around her chest tightened and kept her secure and warm, kept her safe.

The one holding her finally pulled the gas mask off, and she gasped the cool, fresh air into her straining lungs. He brushed the sweat-dampened hair from her brow and placed a soft kiss on her temple.

"How did you like that?" He murmured.

"Amazing," Candee breathed. "So good."

"Glad you enjoyed it, sweetheart. Let's get you some water, and then..."

"And then?"

He smiled. "And then we'll be good for round two."

5 WYOMING WELCOME

There was a bonfire the night Jeremy arrived in the valley, and he followed the bright orange light and the sound of music to the party. There were a few girls, but most of the people gathered around the fire pit were cowboys, taking a night off to unwind with their buddies and a few 30-racks. Jeremy stepped out of the shadows into the circle of light with a friendly smile, introducing himself to the nearest person--a cowboy by the name of Grady. Within minutes, Jeremy was well-acquainted with the group, warming himself by the fire, and enjoying a cold beer. It seemed surreal--almost completely unreal but that was life in Wyoming.

"How long have you been in these parts?" Grady asked, moving to stand at his elbow.

"Just arrived in Star Valley yesterday, I'm staying with some friends."

"Who?"

Jeremy named his buddy from high school--an ex-lover who never understood that Jeremy was actually in love with him. It was funny that he ran to that man for solace now, but everything was so fucked up that Jeremy thought he might be the only friend he had left in this world.

"Ah, yeah, I know him. He's a good man. He's not with you tonight?"

"No, I decided to go exploring on my own. Didn't expect to run into anybody, though I'm sure glad I did. Thanks again, by the way." Jeremy raised his beer in appreciation and Grady shrugged.

"There's plenty to go around. You're just visiting?"

"I don't know," Jeremy answered honestly. "Not much left for me back home. I could get a job out here, live with my buddy for awhile until I find my own place..."

"What's stopping you?"

"Nothing, and yet, too many things to count." As much as he wanted to abandon his life permanently, he knew it would negatively affect, even harm, people he cared about. Normally, that was enough to keep him grounded in reality. But standing there under the universe of stars, warmed inside and out by fire and booze and hospitality, he knew fulfilling his obligations was no longer enough to sustain him. There had to be more in his life than that, and wasn't he ready to find it finally?

"The details," Jeremy finally answered. "Are you from here?"

"No, grew up in Laramie. I moved out here a few years ago."

That seemed like a very minor distinction to Jeremy. "What brought you out here?"

"I was chasing a piece of ass."

"Did she get away?"

"No, I got him, but he didn't want to be caught in the first place. He moved on but I decided to stick around."

The specific use of the masculine pronoun made Jeremy tingle with excitement. Grady was not a bad looking man--he was a few inches shorter than Jeremy's 5'11 frame, with a full, soft beard, smiling brown eyes, and a compact build. He didn't look like much, but Jeremy was used to sizing up other men, and he knew Grady could probably pack one hell of a wallop. Intrigued, he took a small step closer, leaning in so he could feel Grady's body heat.

"Yeah, I've been through the same thing. More than once. You'd think I'd learn by now, but I never do."

Grady smiled companionably and raised his bottle to his lips. Jeremy watched as they fit against the opening, wishing he could knock the beer away. He wanted to claim Grady's mouth, taste the alcohol on his breath and test the texture of his full lips. "You hungry? We have food in those coolers over there. You can help yourself."

"Can I get you anything?"

"Nah, I'm not really hungry."

"Are you sure? Do you even know what's over there? It seems like there's a lot of coolers."

It was a terribly transparent ploy, but it still worked. Grady moved away from the fire and the majority of his friends to the further outskirts of the circle, where the coolers were stacked. Jeremy found bread, cold cuts, and cheese in one, and his stomach growled at the thought of the sandwich he could create. He cleared a spot on the folding picnic table and asked Grady if he wanted one.

"Yeah, thanks. 'preciate it." He watched as Jeremy worked, then accepted the offered sandwich with a smile that made Jeremy a little lightheaded. Suddenly, it wasn't enough to move Grady from the fire and the bulk of the party--he wanted to take Grady off alone somewhere, wanted to kiss him in the absolute darkness of a Wyoming night, lost in the trees and the shadows, silent and shivering together.

"Did you hear that?" Jeremy asked, cocking his head to the side.

"What?" Grady asked, taking another bite from his sandwich.

"That. That right there. Can't you hear it?"

Grady mimicked him, tilting his head as well. "No...maybe it's a bird or something."

"This time of night? I think we should check it out." Another ridiculously transparent ploy. So transparent, in fact, that if Grady went along with it, might that mean he wanted to kiss Jeremy? "It won't take long. Nobody will even notice, I bet."

Grady only nodded, fishing another beer from the ice before gesturing to Jeremy to lead on. Jeremy's heartbeat quickened and his senses were heightened. Luring some strange cowboy into the woods to make a pass at him had never been Jeremy's plan for the night, but he couldn't say he minded. He just hoped he didn't get punched in the face for his effort. They moved deeper and deeper into the woods, until they could only smell, not see, the fire.

"I don't hear anything," Grady finally

said.

He was right. Except for the sound of their steps, there was nothing to hear. The moonlight barely penetrated the canopy of trees, and it almost felt like they were the last two people in the world. Jeremy knew now was the time to make his move, and he acted fast, grabbing Grady by the back of the neck and planting a hard, firm kiss on his full lips. His beard tickled Jeremy's chin, and he felt like he could get drunk from the vapor of booze hanging around Grady's mouth. But the kiss was sweeter than he expected Grady's mouth more pliant and eager, his tongue a surprisingly gentle probe.

Jeremy's instincts took over, his higher brain turning all decisions over to the reptilian base that wanted nothing more than to satisfy hunger. He was more than just hungry. He was absolutely starving for human contact, for an exchange of energy and fluids and breath. After being alone in his own skin for months and months, he was aching to welcome somebody else inside. He didn't know Grady from Adam, but that didn't matter to him. He might not know Grady's heart and mind, but their bodies knew what to do, know how to fan and nurse the sparks between them.

He slammed Grady back to the nearest tree and slid his hands under his arms.

He lifted him off the ground, giving Grady enough clearance to wrap his legs around Jeremy's hips. The kiss deepened, their tongues working against each other furiously while their hands moved like hungry animals over each other. Jeremy tugged at Grady's shirt, pulling the hem free from his jeans and pushing it higher and higher up his chest. Jeremy always liked a hard body--and he was the sort of guy who'd cruise the gym for a good time-- but Grady's body was unlike anything he'd ever touched. It wasn't the product of the focused training of the gym, but rather the constant realities of his life. Jeremy had lifted him like he weighed nothing, but with his palms spread over Grady's chest, he knew the man had serious strength. The thought was enough to make Jeremy shiver with fresh delight, his cock swelling to complete hardness.

They moved with each other, working as the perfect team to get their shirts off and their pants undone. In the dim light, his dark skin was almost invisible, except where Grady touched him. Their tones were a sharp contrast, and Jeremy loved the sight of his chocolate fingers on Grady's creamy skin. He kissed Grady's mouth hard enough to bruise his lips, then tore his mouth away and continued his exploration. Grady's beard was as soft as it looked against his mouth, and the skin beneath his ear smelled magnificent. Jeremy couldn't put his finger on exactly what comprised the scent, but it reminded him of camping in the early spring and freshly brewed coffee at dawn.

Jeremy lifted Grady higher, securing Grady's legs beneath his armpits. Grady's thick dick jutted from his open fly, and Jeremy's mouth watered as he lowered his head to the crown between his lips. Grady moaned at that contact, and Jeremy kissed the hot, throbbing flesh, peppering the skin with tiny pecks before closing his mouth around the bulbous head. Grady reached up to the branch overhead, gripping it tightly and jutting his hips forward, pushing himself even deeper. Jeremy dropped his jaw open and bobbed his head down, taking the tip of his long cock all the way to the back of his throat. He stopped there for a long second, closing his eyes and simply breathing, allowing himself to feel the weight of Grady's desire resting against his tongue. A cool breeze whispered over them, but the heat from Grady's body and his own flush of passion kept the chills away.

Jeremy wasn't in any sort of hurry. He could hold Grady up against that tree all night and in all of Wyoming there was nothing half as interesting or delicious as Grady's cock. He moved his head in a lazy rhythm, stopping often to wrap his tongue around the shaft or dip the tip into his leaking hole. Salt was like a magnet for his tongue, and he went after every drop and smear of pre-come. And then, when the crown was clean of the salty goodness, he drove his head lower and lower, until his nose was buried in the curly hair at the base of his dick. There he inhaled pure pheromones, getting high off them. Grady moved his hips, swinging them back and forth, rocking side to side, his strong arms flexing, muscles bulging as he hung from the branch.

Jeremy surrendered to the pleasure pulsing through him, doing only what felt good, and prolonging that sensation for as long as he could. Grady's cock was a feast of delights for him, and he gave himself permission to learn every centimeter of the terrain, following veins with his tongue, finding small dips in the otherwise flawless, smooth skin. He might have continued on like that all night, but Grady's hips began to move with new enthusiasm, shifting his legs to hook them over Jeremy's shoulders, wrapping them around his head in a tight hold, burying Jeremy's face firmly against his groin. With his head stuck in place, Grady slammed his hips forward, burying himself deep in Jeremy's throat. They moaned in unison--Jeremy's muffled and Grady's a high pitched sound of relief.

He jerked his hips, humping himself against Jeremy's face faster and faster. Jeremy pressed his palms into the small of Grady's back, holding him but unable to stop him or control him in anyway. He fucked Jeremy's face with utter abandon, completely selfish and self-centered, focused entirely on the sharp pleasure slicing through him. Jeremy didn't mind. He kept his jaw relaxed and his throat opened, more than happy to let Grady fuck his face and pounded his dick down Jeremy's throat. He couldn't move his head, couldn't break away from the prison of Grady's legs. He was locked in place, gagging and huffing for breath while Grady brutalized his mouth. His own cock bobbed freely, the throbbing flesh sending an ache all the way through his groin to the pit of his stomach. He desperately needed to feel a hand or, even better, a mouth fit around his dick.

But at the moment, he was helpless to do anything about that. Grady's balls brushed against his chin, and his breath came in harsher and harsher gasps. Jeremy knew he was getting close, and he slicked Grady's dick with fresh spit at the thought of swallowing down his cum. He gripped Grady's ass, his finger squeezing and kneading the surprisingly ample flesh. He pulled the cheeks apart and let his fingertips skim over Grady's pucker. Grady sucked in his breath sharply at the contact and rocked back, pushing on Jeremy's finger. He let his digit slip past the tight ring of muscle, pushing it deep into the tight, clenching channel. Grady moaned and shifted his hips; his muscles clenching so tightly that Jeremy couldn't move his hand.

"Almost...almost..." Grady panted.

Jeremy knew exactly what he was missing, what he was waiting for, and he managed to twist his hand, grinding his finger against the tender prostate. Grady howled in response, his hips jerking wildly as he flooded Jeremy's throat with thick cum. Jeremy's throat worked as he swallowed it down, milking Grady of every last bit. Gradually, his hips slowed and then finally stopped. After a few breaths, he unwrap his legs from Jeremy's neck, allowing him to step back. Grady hung from the branch for another moment, his softening cock at eye-level. Jeremy almost reached for him again, but Grady dropped from the branch, landing as softly as a cat in a low crouch. He shifted from a crouch to his knees, darting his head forward to swallow Jeremy's cock down to the root.

With the taste of Grady still fresh on his

tongue and the sounds of his orgasm still echoing in his ears, the sudden pressure of Grady's mouth was almost enough to send him right over the edge. He put a hand out, catching himself on the tree, pressing his thin skin into the tree's rough bark. The pain brought him back, allowed him to catch him just before losing it completely. Grady didn't allow him to keep that control for very long, though. He hollowed his cheeks, creating a tight seal around Jeremy's shaft, and moved his head in a hard, fast rhythm, with the same energy and force as he used to move his hips. Once again, Jeremy found he couldn't resist the other man's will or his strength, both wrapping around him like a tornado, shaking him where he stood.

Pleasure sprung in him, whipping through him like a high-tension wire. He shook, vibrating from the inside out as he spilled his load in Grady's accepting throat. The pleasure was intense, but his relief afterwards was even more so, literally knocking his knees out from beneath him. Somehow, Grady caught him, lowering him to the ground before he could fall.

"You have a great dick," Grady said with warm appreciation.

Jeremy blinked up at him. "So do you."

"I don't know what you're looking for or what you're thinking this is...but you know, if you want to bunk with me tonight, I wouldn't be opposed."

Jeremy wouldn't bunk with him--but he would follow him back to wherever he called home and fuck him until the sun came up. Grady had no problem with that.

6 WYOMING HOSPITALITY
Wyoming Welcome 2

Grady had a trailer in the park on the edge of town. A nice double-wide that he kept clean and orderly. He gestured vaguely as they stepped through the door, indicating Jeremy should make himself home. He sank into the comfortable couch and looked around, taking in the full details of his new environment. He saw the man in a million little details, and he found himself touched to be invited back to his sanctuary. This wasn't just a place he bedded down when he was in town. Only a counter separated the kitchen from the living room, and his eyes came to a rest on Grady's back as he fished two cold beers from the fridge.

"I like your place. It's nice."

"Thanks. It's not much but I like it."

"Not much?" Jeremy shook his head. "It looks like you've got it all." He was being serious. He couldn't think of what more a man would need than what Grady had right out there on display. It felt like he was a rich man compared to the destitution of Jeremy's life. He took the beer from Grady and patted the cushion beside him. Grady joined him right away and tucked in close. Jeremy put his arm over his shoulders and sighed at the warmth, at the comfort he found there. Maybe this was all false and he was fooling himself, but at the moment, it felt like he'd found a balm for his troubled heart and the answer to his most desperate prayer. They sat in silence for a long time, drinking from their beers and simply absorbing each other's warmth.

Grady was the first to move, head brushing against Jeremy's shoulder as he looked up. Jeremy glanced down at the same time, and their lips were perfectly angled for a connection. They moved at the same time, Grady lifting his arm and hooking his hand around the back of Jeremy's head to hold him firmly against his mouth. He can still taste himself on Grady's mouth, but there's other things there too, the beer and the smoke from the bonfire and his own personal taste. It all popped across Jeremy's tongue, making his taste buds tingle, electricity bursting down his throat to heat his stomach. Within seconds of the beginning of the kiss, he was hard again and his hand was traveling down Grady's chest. He came to a rest on the bulge in Grady's jeans, evidence that he wasn't the only one turned topsy-turvy by the kiss.

Grady moaned and turned his body into Jeremy's, rising up on one knee to throw his leg over Jeremy's lap. Jeremy took him by the hips and pulled him snugly against his crotch, spreading his legs wide to cradle him. He sank back against the couch, opening to Grady's tongue every time he licked over Jeremy's swollen lips. Jeremy lost track of time as they kissed. It was just like being a little kid again, when a bright summer day could pass in a blink of an eye, and a dark winter night could last for a year. His hands roamed over Jeremy's body, tugging and pulling at his clothes until he finally had his shirt opened and pushed off his shoulders. Grady helped with the process, but he refused to break his mouth from Jeremy's. That connection clouded his brain, and each long, slow sensual kiss touched him in ways, in places, that he hadn't felt in a very long time.

Grady's hands were busy too and he expertly popped open the buttons down

Jeremy's shirt, shoving it off his arms and opening his skin to Grady's rough caresses. There was nothing gentle about his touch. His skin was calloused and there was so much strength in his hands. He pressed his fingers and palms down on Jeremy's shoulders and chest, forcing past the resistance of his tense and tender muscles. His muscles bunched up automatically, but Grady only pressed harder, until the knots straightened and the pressure that plagued his shoulders and neck began to ease. He felt a difference from the joint of his jaw all the way down to the movement of his fingers.

"God, that's amazing," Jeremy said against his lips.

"You're so tense. What have you been carrying? The weight of the world?"

"That's what it feels like."

Grady rocked back, grinding his ass into Jeremy's erection. The tight jeans bit down on his skin and his moan was a strangled plea and protest all at once. Grady apparently knew exactly what that meant, and he slid his long fingers between their bodies, pulling his fly open and fishing Jeremy's cock free from his underwear. Grady fisted him, moaning slightly as his fingers closed around his shaft. Jeremy's eyes rolled back in his head with pleasure and relief. It had only been an hour, at the most, since he sank into the heat of Grady's mouth, but it felt like at least a decade since anybody touched him. He was tender and touchy, sensitive with every flick of Grady's thumb, and his slit enthusiastically leaked pre-cum.

"You're so sensitive."

"It's you," Jeremy choked out.

"Hope you're not too sensitive. I have some plans for you."

"Oh, what in particular?"

"Wait here. I'll be right back."

Jeremy groaned as Grady jumped from his lap, taking away the delightful heat of his body and the maddening but wonderful pressure against his dick. He disappeared into the bedroom at the end of the hall, returning with a condom and a bottle of lube.

"In particular, I want you to fuck me."

"Okay," Jeremy breathed, his cock bobbing in agreement.

Grady didn't know what it was about Jeremy, but from the moment he laid his eyes on the other man he wanted him. There wasn't any question or hesitation. Grady didn't believe in pining. If you wanted something bad enough, you went after it, and he wanted Jeremy bad enough to go to any lengths. He was obviously a good-looking man, beautiful even, with smooth chocolate skin and thick muscles across his chest. He was well-developed everywhere, hard and enticing. Truly a sight to behold in his tight blue jeans and black button down shirt. He walked into the center of light like he already owned the place, and since Grady didn't even sense his approach, it was easy to think he was some demon, or maybe some angel, sent to lure Grady right into temptation.

If that was the case, then mission accomplished. Grady was caught up in the trap of temptation and completely lost there. Getting his dick sucked hadn't been enough. Letting Jeremy slide down his throat wasn't enough. The only thing even remotely sort of satisfying was the burn of Jeremy's finger in his ass, and it was all he could think about as they drove back to his trailer. He knew exactly how that big black cock would feel as it split him open, and his fingers shook with anticipation. His whole body seemed to be trembling, and he was amazed that he could support his own weight as he walked to the bedroom and back.

He shucked the rest of his clothes and helped Jeremy shed his, then tore the condom open with his teeth. He held it between his thumb and forefinger and dropped to his knees, catching Jeremy's cock and guiding it back to his mouth. He sank up and down slowly, this time keeping his eyes fixed on Jeremy. It had been too dark to see his reaction before, and now he was glad he took the time to read his face. His eyes fluttered close and his mouth parted and so much of the tension he sensed in Jeremy's body evaporated from his face that he looked much younger, and somehow even more gorgeous. Grady's heart twisted and his groin pulled tight. God, he wanted this man. Where did he come from? Who the hell was he? Would he even be around the next day? The first question was the only one that really mattered, and Grady didn't even care too much, as long as he got to feel Jeremy's cock in his ass. That was all the information or answers he needed.

He made Jeremy's cock slick with pre-cum and spit before lifting his head. He rolled the condom down his length and then added a thick layer of lube. He stood, reaching behind him with his slick fingers, spreading the lube over his pucker before pushing forward, filling his length with two fingers. He pumped them in and out, making his walls as slick as possible before straddling Jeremy's lap again.

"Is that going to be enough prep?"

Grady nodded. It had been a few years since he last met somebody he wanted this much, but he fucked himself open on a regular basis with his dildo. His ass was more than prepared for the embarrassment of the riches before him. His toy was a little bit bigger than Jeremy, but it wasn't just about size. He wanted the heat and the power, he wanted to be held and pounded, and he wanted to go for a ride. Jeremy's dick felt like a steel rod pressing against his opening, hard and slick and more than ready to impale him.

Grady forced himself to take it slow. He wanted to take all of Jeremy in a single hard thrust, but this required a bit more care and control than that, and he slid down an inch at a time. Jeremy pressed his fingers against his back, holding him lightly as Grady gained more and more depth. Their mouths connected again, the kiss starting as slow as before, but growing more and more heated as Grady's body stretched to accommodate Jeremy's impressive width. He sucked Jeremy's tongue into his mouth to keep from shouting with pleasure as he finally reached the bottom of his shaft and felt Jeremy's balls brush against his ass. Their tongues dueled and fought while Grady struggled to catch his breath and adjust to the amazingly exquisite pressure.

"Do you want to move or shall I?"

Grady moaned and straightened his

legs, rising up on his knees. He dropped back, rose up, dropped back, forcing a grunt from Jeremy each time he came down. He didn't want to rock, didn't want to keep Jeremy buried inside. He wanted to feel every centimeter, sliding in and out and burning with every second. His pleasure built quickly, but he found the perfect threshold, keeping himself there with the careful control of the rhythm, holding himself back from the edge with well-practiced control.

Jeremy was about to lose his ever-loving mind. Everything about Grady was amazing. His well-muscled, compact body, the way he moved and flexed, the beautiful expression of pleasure stamping his features, the precision of his hips. He squeezed tight with each downward stroke, the pressure around his aching shaft so intense that he didn't know how he wasn't already broken. Every inch, every second, was better than the one before it, and he was drowning in kisses. He couldn't hold Grady close enough or tight enough, couldn't taste enough of his mouth. He let Grady control the rhythm entirely, more than happy to let him take what he needed, let him do anything he wanted.

But eventually he felt a certain quiver in Grady's thighs and a certain twitch in his hips. He spanned his fingers over his slender waist, curving his fingers to the back and pulling him back until he was nearly horizontal, his back resting on Jeremy's knees, his body stretched out for Jeremy's pleasure. He was fascinated by the way his muscles shifted beneath his skin, and by the way his hair covered his pecks and narrowed to a tiny trail down his stomach to the patch of black curls at the base of his cock. He urged Grady back further and then slammed him down, taking over the rhythm with a hard declaration. Grady moaned, his ass clenching and fluttering around Jeremy's dick.

"Ready?" Jeremy breathed.

Grady's eyes flew open, meeting Jeremy's, and he nodded his head once. Jeremy put his heels flat against the floor and hoisted his hips up, distributing his weight between his feet and his shoulders as he pounded into Grady's ass. His strokes were long and powerful and fast, more than enough to steal Grady's breath from his lungs, though Jeremy never even panted. Everything about his body, from his strokes to his breathing, remained under tight control and in perfect rhythm. He could literally do this all night, now that the first one was rubbed out. He could fuck Grady until he passed out, and then keep fucking him until he woke up again, and then go for another hour after that.

He wasn't sure if Grady realized what he'd done, recognized the beast he woke in Jeremy, but he definitely seemed game for the ride. Sweat glistened over his skin, made Jeremy slick, made their skin clap with more force every time they slammed together. He wasn't sure, but he almost felt like the trailer itself was rocking from the force of their coupling. The harder he fucked, the more Grady seemed to love it. He grew more and more vocal, his shouts and yelps telling Jeremy everything he needed to know.

Without missing a stroke, Jeremy stood and carried him over to the nearest wall. He slammed him back hard enough to rattle the windows, and the new angle hit exactly where Jeremy hoped it would. Grady's eyes flew open, and his shock was silent and almost comedic. Jeremy grinned and slammed his dick into the delicate bundle of nerves, hitting the prostate with all the force, all the strength in his body. He screamed on the third stroke and then he burst with the fourth, his cock going off like a fountain, painting Jeremy's chest with the warm liquid. That didn't even slow him down. He slammed forward again and again, forcing even more fluid from him.

"Oh God...oh God...oh God God...oh oh oh oh oh FUCK!" Then the words fell away into panting moans that sounded almost like pleas. Almost like he wanted Jeremy to stop and let him catch his breath. But that wasn't going to happen. Not until he got his fill of Grady's ass. Not until he couldn't take one more second without literally, physically breaking.

Grady claimed his mouth, and the pleas transferred from touch to touch, lip to lip, without a single sound. Jeremy groaned, pushed himself harder and harder until they were both panting and his control seemed more like a fairy tale he told himself. When the frayed edges finally snapped he positioned in one final time and exploded, the condom catching what felt like a gallon of jizz.

He stumbled backwards to the couch, fell down, groaned as that only pushed his softening cock deeper. Grady answered his groan and collapsed forward, resting his head on Jeremy's shoulder while he gasped for the oxygen that they both needed.

7 BUT IT'S ALRIGHT

"It's alright, it's alright girl. Oooooh, it's alright! Alright girl! You hurt me once, you hurt me twice, but it's alright...alright girl..." Gavin's booming voice faded as he stumbled into the house, but he was still loud enough to pull Leon from a deep sleep. He moaned and rolled over, trying to bury his head in his pillow and shut out the sound of Gavin's off-key singing, but the walls were too thin and Gavin was too drunk.

"It's alright, alright girl. You hurting me, but it's alright. Alright girl. Oooooh, it's alright."

"Fuck, doesn't he know any other song?" He reached for the nearest heavy object and threw it at the bedroom door, the sudden crash startling Gavin out of his song. "Hey! Shut the fuck up!"

Blessed silence descended and Leon collapsed back to his pillow with a sigh of relief. His relief was short-lived, though. In the next minute, the door swung open and Gavin stood silhouetted against the hall light. "Did you say something?" He slurred.

"Yeah, I told you to shut the fuck up."

"Oh. Oh, I'm sorry, dude. I've just had this goddamned song stuck in my head all night." He bent over, clutching his head like the goddamned song was trying to spring from his brow, and then shot straight up, belting the words out again. "You keep hurting me, but it's alright. It's alright, alright dear. Oooh, it's alright."

"I swear to god, I'm going to break your fucking head if you don't stop that."

"What? Don't you think it's a great song?"

"It's a damned annoying song. And you're a damned terrible singer."

"Sorry. I didn't mean to offend your sensibilities." Gavin grinned, and Leon didn't think he was sorry at all. He also wasn't leaving. He was just standing there, grinning like a dope.

"Go to bed before you do yourself any damage," Leon said, rolling over onto his side and tucking the pillow under his chin.

"I'm not sleepy."

"You're drunk. That's close enough to sleepy," Leon bit back.

"You sound annoyed."

"I am annoyed. Some of us have to work in the morning. Did you happen to see what time it is?"

Gavin tilted his head, eyes narrowing as he did the math. "I know I was around for last call, so it must be...three in the goddamned morning. Fuck. I got all caught up in that song."

"Go plug in your iPod or something. Just...get the fuck out of my room and let me sleep."

Instead of leaving, Gavin came in and threw himself on the foot of the bed, his normally smiling face pulled into a long frown. Leon tried to ignore him, but it was impossible to ignore the heavy frown on his face. Gavin wasn't a frowner. He had a smile at all times, for everybody, and for the first time, Leon felt a twinge of genuine concern under the layers of irritation.

"What happened?"

"Nothing."

"Come on. You can tell me." And he obviously wanted to talk, so really he should stop wasting their time. The minutes were ticking by, and Leon still hoped to get back to sleep before his alarm went off at 5:30.

"It's Nina."

"What's Nina?"

"The problem. My life. Everything." He waved his hand and dropped it back to his side. "It's Nina."

"Did she break up with you?" Leon hunted the corners of his memory, but he couldn't remember one thing about this Nina. He'd never heard of her, never met her.

"No, no, no. I met her tonight."

"Ah."

"And she's beautiful. Radiant. Perfect. She gave me her number. But then I saw her dancing with another guy and I just...sort of lost it."

"Did you pick a fight with some random guy over a girl?"

"May have."

"Jesus Christ, Gavin. Where's your head at? Did anybody get hurt?" What he really wanted to know is if the police would be knocking on their door with a warrant for Gavin's arrest.

"No, nobody was hurt." His smile was almost sheepish. "I may have been a bit deep in my cups. I didn't actually connect with him, but Nina...ooh, she was pissed. She didn't care that her precious Ronald walked away unscathed." His face twisted with disgust and then instantly crumpled under fresh misery. "She told me to lose her number."

"Well, Romeo and Juliet this is not. Go

to bed, get some sleep, and in the morning....what the fuck are you doing?"

Gavin kicked his pants to the floor and pulled the duvet up, diving under the cover with a boyish smile. "Going to bed."

"Not my bed."

"Yes, your bed."

"No, Gavin."

"Yes, Leon." He took Leon by the shoulder and gently pulled him backwards. "It's the least I can do after I woke you up and bored you with my ridiculous sob story."

"You don't have to do anything. And I don't want it just because you think you owe me," Leon said, trying to pull away from his surprisingly tight grip. "Seriously."

"Fine, maybe I just want to. Did that ever occur to you?" He pushed Leon down to the mattress and moved quickly, swinging his leg over Leon's torso and settling his ass against Leon's--admittedly interested--cock. "Maybe I like to feel your monster of a cock, and maybe I like the taste of you, and maybe...maybe I knew my singing would wake you up."

"And maybe you acted like a drunken jerk because you really wanted to lose her number?"

Gavin's grin returned. "Now you're getting it." He smoothed his hands up and down Leon's muscled torso, looking as happy as a little boy in a candy store. Leon tried to pretend like he didn't enjoy every second of contact, but when Gavin's fingers trailed over his nipples, his mask cracked a little. Gavin circled the pink discs until the tips started to harden, standing at eager attention for Gavin's hot mouth. He rotated his hips, grinding his ass down on Leon's dick, coaxing more and more blood to his groin. His cock nudged at Gavin's pucker, slipping between his hot cheeks while his pretty cock dripped with fresh pre-cum.

Leon wrapped his fingers around the velvet smooth skin of his shaft, a soft sigh escaping him as he stroked Gavin's impressive length. He wasn't as long as Leon, and certainly not as thick, but he was still quite remarkable. Leon lifted himself up on his elbows, bending forward to catch the tip of his hard dick, sucking the clear fluid from the tip. Gavin groaned, his knees squeezing around Leon's ribs while he pushed himself up, guiding more of his length into Leon's hot mouth. Gavin reached down, fisting Leon's long, curly hair, his fingers flexing and pulling until Leon's scalp tingled.

"God, you've got the best mouth. Feels so fucking good..." Words fell from Gavin's mouth, mostly unheard and unheeded. He was always talking, always sharing, and always inviting people into the intimacy of his thoughts and feelings. It used to bother Leon, but he was used to it now. So used to it that when he fucked people who kept their sounds to a few moans and whimpers it felt strange. Like something was missing.

He hollowed his cheeks, sucking hard on Gavin's cock, his own dick throbbing to the rhythm he created with his bobbing head. But he couldn't get enough of Gavin at that angle. He wanted to feel his thick cock all the way down his throat. He sat up and wrapped his arms around Gavin, tilting him backwards. Gavin unbent his legs, sticking them straight out as Leon put him on his back and bent over him, ticking the sensitive tip with his ginger whiskers. Gavin rolled his hips and Leon dropped his mouth open, swallowing him down in a single stroke, burying his nose against Leon's belly. His throat stretched to accommodate the thick meat, and for once, Gavin was silent. Leon smiled to himself--that trick always worked. Gavin was just incapable of talking when he had his dick completely buried inside of Leon.

Leon moved like he had all the time in the world, drawing out each sensation until Gavin was jerking his hips and whimpering. He made the sweetest little sounds when he was really into it, each one going directly to Leon's cock. His balls throbbed, his eyeballs rolled, and his muscles were tight, ready to be unleashed. That was his sign to slip his hand beneath Gavin's ass, seeking his tight opening. The pucker gave easily to Leon's probing finger, and he slipped it in up to the knuckle. Gavin gasped, his legs falling open even wider like the little slut he was. Leon moved his finger with his mouth, sliding in as he took Gavin's dick down his throat, easing out as he lifted his head. He started slow at first; specifically trying to drive Gavin insane, but it didn't take long to forget that game, too caught up in his own needs to play. He moved his mouth and his finger faster and faster, not thinking about anything except Gavin's moans and whimpers, until the hand in his hair squeezed hard enough to yank his head up.

"I'm...I'm going to cum dude..." Gavin panted.

Leon pulled away from him and hunted for a condom in his nightstand. Fortunately, there was still one in the top drawer, and he didn't lose any time ripping it from the foil and unrolling it down his dick. He poured a liberal amount of lube over his shaft and his fingers, spreading it from the tip to the base before seeking Gavin's ass with his slick fingers. He pushed two inside of him, spreading the lube as deeply as he could, rotating his wrist in half-circles to stretch Gavin's channel. Gavin made breathless, encouraging sounds, urging Leon to fuck him, to please fuck him, to fuck him with his big monster dick.

Leon was happy to oblige him, more than eager to get his cock buried in the welcoming heat of Gavin's ass. He held the back of Gavin's knees, forcing his legs up and out wide, exposing his slick asshole. Gavin's hands went to the back of his thighs, holding himself up as Leon guided the tip of his dick to Gavin's opening. They'd done this so many times that Leon knew exactly how it would feel to breach the flesh and slide into the tight channel, but somehow it always took him by surprise. He fucked lots of people, but he never fucked anybody who felt quite so good; like his ass had been specifically designed for Leon's cock. Sliding into him was like sliding a sword into its hilt--it just belonged.

Once he was fully seated, Gavin let his legs close around Leon, and Leon dropped forward, holding himself above Gavin's body on outstretched arms. His muscles bulged and flexed as he moved, slowly sliding his hips back, moving in and out of Gavin with long, sure strokes. Gavin's eyes stayed locked on Leon's until he couldn't take it anymore and he slammed their mouths together, kissing Gavin like he knew he shouldn't. Getting naked with him, sucking his dick, fucking him--all those things were acceptable. But kissing? Kissing was never a good idea. Gavin liked it too much and Leon...well, Leon liked it, too. He liked the way his mouth fit against Gavin's wide lips, and he liked the taste of booze on his breath. He liked Gavin's bold tongue, the feeling of his soft mustache tickling his nose, and the way they sort of melted together, like their mouths were made of overheated wax.

Leon didn't let anything disrupt his deliberate, careful rhythm. He wanted to feel every inch of Gavin's delicious body gripping him on the way out and then on the way in again. He wanted to feel his lean body flex, his hard muscles fluttering and moving beneath the perfection of his skin. Once they started kissing, Gavin wouldn't let him go, his hand a steel trap on the back of Leon's head. When he tried to pull away for breath, Gavin chased his mouth, catching him again almost before he could inhale fresh oxygen. But that was okay. Leon was used to the way Gavin made his head--and everything else--spin in rapid circles.

He slipped his hand between their bodies, his fingers closing around Gavin's dick. He stroked him with a harder, faster rhythm, pulling helpless moans from deep in Gavin's throat. He even tried to push Leon's hand away from his shaft, but Leon wouldn't loosen his grip for anything. Not even the end of the world. He stroked faster and faster, purposefully winding up Gavin's body, making him tighter around Leon's aching flesh.

"I'm going...oh fuck Leon...Leon, buddy, you have to...gotta stop."

"Why?" Leon rasped.

"I don't want to...not right now...not yet..."

"You don't want to cum?" Leon smiled a little before dipping his head to bite at the tender flesh at the base of Gavin's throat. That was dirty pool, and he knew it. Gavin was supremely sensitive there, and the smallest scrape of Leon's teeth could send him into convulsions of pleasure. This was more than a scrape, though. He caught the skin between his teeth and bit down, sucking at the same time to pull his blood to the surface even faster, quickly forming a large hickey.

"Oh...fuck!" Gavin's hips went crazy, slamming back and forth while he shot his load all over Leon's hands in spurt after spurt. Leon milked him for every strand, spreading the slick liquid up and down Gavin's softening cock. He whimpered, bearing down on Leon's cock, slamming his ass against Leon hard enough to make a sharp cracking sound every time their flesh met.

"Come on," Gavin panted. "Come on, I

want your load."

Leon shuddered, pulling his dick free of Gavin's ass and ripping the condom off. Gavin knew what he wanted, and he obediently opened his mouth, allowing Leon to feed him all the way down his throat. Gavin gripped his ass, his fingers sinking in the flesh of Leon's ass as he tried to pull him even deeper. Leon rocked back and forth, pumping his hips faster and faster until the friction and the tight heat got to be too much for him. His balls pulled tight, prepared to empty themselves entirely, the cum shooting straight down Gavin's throat to his stomach. He held himself deep inside until he stopped twitching, his dick spent of every drop.

He fell backwards and to the side, collapsing on the mattress as the last of his strength drained from his muscles. Gavin remained motionless, but Leon could tell by the sound of his breathing that he was quite satisfied with their coupling.

"Now you going to let me get some sleep?"

"After that, I'll do you one better."

"Yeah?"

"I'll make you breakfast so you can get a little extra sleep."

Leon's lips twitched. It was a fine sentiment, but Leon didn't believe it for a second. Once Gavin passed out, he'd sleep until all the booze had been metabolized. But he really did appreciate the sentiment, and he didn't have any problem slipping back into dreamland.

8 LATE NIGHT SNACK

Sara has never met Jeff, and now the golden child has returned to the family fold. It's a huge deal, and she has no idea what to expect of the man who has such a huge role in her husband's, Phil, life. Nobody loves Jeff like Phil, and he wants nothing more than his wife and his brother to get along. The problem is that from the second they meet, they do get along. Far, far too well. Can either one of them resist the temptation or is their desire already too close to betrayal?

The house was in a tizzy, caught up in a flurry of activity since early that morning. The entire Jensen family was descending on the old family home, eager to celebrate the return of their favored son, Jeff. He'd been away for several years, first at school, then traveling, and then a surprise stint with the Marines that nobody could explain, not even Jeff, who never offered more than a shrug and a "It seemed like the right thing to do." But now, he was discharged and coming home, and nobody who knew him wanted to miss that.

Unfortunately for Sara, she did not know him. She met and married Phil, his younger brother, while he was away in Afghanistan. She'd seen pictures of him and she could probably pick him out of a crowd, but she didn't know his smile, never heard his laugh, and definitely didn't understand the man's natural charisma and huge appeal. She didn't think much about it, either, but Phil was clearly nervous about something. He had a dozen little tells when he was anxious, and every single one made an appearance before breakfast. She tried to calm him, tried to reassure him before they left the bedroom—his old room that still had most of his adolescent decorations, a beacon of boyish preteen innocence. But he would not be reassured, though he gave her a smile that was meant to reassure her. She didn't understand his concern, to be honest. She was married to him; what would she want with a stranger who happened to be his brother?

Breakfast was a loud, noisy affair with four generations of the Jensen family crammed into the kitchen and the dining room, ranging from eight months to eighty years. The kids couldn't be quieted, and the adults couldn't be distracted from their conversations, their memories, and their excitement. Sara kept to herself, listening with half an ear while Phil and his sister Beth reminisced about when they were kids and Jeff was their fearless leader in all kinds of adventures. It sounded like they would have followed their older brother to hell, if it came to that, and Sara wondered why Phil didn't do just that and enlist when he learned Jeff was being shipped out. She made a note to ask him later and went back to picking at her waffles.

A key turned in the door and everybody moved at once. Sara had never seen anything like it, and she hung back, happy to stay out of the way of the stampede. She'd meet him either way, and she didn't need to be in the way of hugs and tears and kisses and more tears and then even more hugs. She heard the commotion of his arrival from the dining room, smiling to herself at the various laughs and shrieks and manly "How you doing bro?" type of questions. After ten minutes or so, she heard Phil's familiar laugh and then, "Sara must still be in the kitchen. Come on, I can't wait for you to meet her."

Sara delicately wiped her lips, brushed the toast crumbs from her shirt, stood as they entered, and then promptly forgot everything about her life including her own name. In the face of such stunning, unexpected, amazing beauty, it was amazing she could even remember how to breathe. He was taller than Phil by at least a half foot, his cheeks, nose, and jaw as sharp as Phil's was stubbed. Phil was cute, attractive, and fun to be with, but his brother was a God walking among men. Then he smiled, and her heart did a weird little jitter-shake.

"Sara, it's such a pleasure to meet you. I swear, Phil talks about you so much, I know your life story." He put his hand out and she really didn't want to take it, but she couldn't snub him. How would she ever explain that to Phil? 'I didn't shake your brother's hand because I was worried there mere touch of his skin would soak my panties.' It didn't. But the sudden brush of his lips across her cheek made her weak in the knees, and the way he held her hand was like a revelation. She never wanted to take her palm away, never wanted to break the tenuous connection between them.

"The pleasure's mine. I've heard a lot about you, too."

"All good, I hope."

"I was under the impression there

wasn't anything but good things to say about you."

Jeff laughed. "Yeah, well, you know what they say about absence. Give it a week and you'll be hearing about what a terrible bastard I am."

She laughed, but she didn't believe him. The rest of the family trooped in, and breakfast was resumed, this time with Jeff at the head of the table with a huge plate of food. Sara returned to her seat, but any interest she had in the food was long gone. She made a show of eating her waffles, though, and hoped nobody (especially her husband) noticed the way she couldn't take her eyes off Jeff's perfect face.

There was no hope of getting a single second alone with Jeff, which was just as well because Sara didn't really need the temptation in her life. She kept to herself while the family talked, played games, drank beer, and generally indulged in the big celebration that was Jeff's homecoming. Sometimes, she thought he might be looking back at her, but she was sure that wasn't the case. If it ever seemed like he was, it was only her imagination. Still, the one time she was sure she caught his gaze traveling over her body, she blushed a teenaged shade of pink and excused herself from the room.

That night, after everybody went to bed and the house was completely silent, she was still awake. Still staring at the ceiling and listening to her husband's light snoring and thinking about Jeff. All of the details of his life seemed worthy of her attention. She tried to push him out of her thoughts, she truly did, but it was never that easy. He intruded, piggy-backed on innocent thoughts, lurked in the back of her mind and sprang at the most unexpected times. She tried to tell herself it would all be okay, but she didn't quite believe that, either. It wasn't as though she only had to get through the weekend. Jeff was back in town for good, and Phil loved his older brother deeply. This was something she'd be plagued with forever unless she got it under control.

Sighing, she slipped out of bed and into her robe and slippers. Maybe a glass of warm milk or a walk around the block would help. Maybe she'd nick a cigarette from her mother-in-law—she hadn't smoked in years, but she'd never felt like this before and maybe nicotine was exactly what she needed to calm her nerves. The kitchen was as empty and dark as she expected, and she crossed the tiled room without a sound to pull the fridge open.

"You couldn't sleep either, huh?"

Sara nearly jumped out of her skin. Spinning around with a hand clutching at her heart, she saw Jeff's amused smile. She opened the fridge wider, allowing a larger rectangle of light to fall over the kitchen, revealing he was in the middle of a rather impressive midnight snack.

"Oh my god, you scared me half to death."

"Sorry 'bout that. I thought you saw me here."

"No....no, I was distracted." By thoughts of him. The irony wasn't lost on her. "You're still hungry?"

"Yeah...I never got enough food overseas. And nobody cooks like Mom. You want some?" He offered her the dish of pie that he was stabbing at with a fork. He hadn't bothered removing the pastry from the pan even though there was more than enough to share.

"Yeah, thanks. This pie is delicious. Old family recipe?"

"As far as I know. Don't know where she found it, just know that nobody ever makes apple pies like her."

"I'd ask her for the recipe, but I don't think she'd give it to me."

Jeff laughed at that. A big, good-natured sound that told her he knew exactly what she was talking about. For the first time, it seemed like Jeff might prove himself worthy of being more than a distraction—he might actually be an ally in the crazy world of the Jensen family. "Oh...you've got something on the corner of your mouth."

"Oops. Here?" She brushed at the left side.

"No."

"Here?" The right side.

"Nope, not quite. Here, let me."

She held herself perfectly still as he leaned over, careful not to flinch away when he actually touched her. Even more careful to not lean in the touch. She was as stiff and still as a tree as he wiped the crumb away. The brush of his finger still made her tingle. "Got it."

She couldn't resist licking the spot he touched. Was it her imagination or could she taste a hint of his aftershave? "Thanks."

"No problem. Do you mind if I ask you a question? And please know, I don't mean any disrespect at all. I'm just curious."

"Sure. Ask away."

"How did a woman like you end up with my baby brother? He's a great guy, and I love him but...you're a little out of his league, aren't you?"

Sara laughed. "No offense taken. Most people think the same thing, though they aren't his most beloved brother, so I guess none of them feel safe enough to say it. But I liked Phil from the first moment I met him. He's genuine and he's sweet and I know I can trust him. I do trust him. And he trusts me." The last sentence was more for her own sake than for Jeff's.

"I guess I'm not used to most people looking at him and seeing what I see."

"Maybe most women can't see him at all around you."

Jeff's lips quirked. "Maybe. You know, it's funny. He probably didn't do it on purpose, but he managed to find and marry the one woman I would say is just my type."

"Is that a fact?"

Jeff leaned closer. "Very much so."

Sara's brain was screaming at her to leave, to get out of the kitchen, and go back to her husband, who was asleep and secure in the knowledge that his wife was "his." But...a part of him must have known this would happen. She supposed that was the source of all his anxiety. He knew Sara would be attractive to his brother, and of course, Jeff was attractive to everybody who had eyes. Knowing how much he feared this very thing, she could not justify sitting in that chair for another second.

But she didn't get up. She didn't pull away when Jeff leaned closer. She even let him touch her mouth, her oxygen rushing out of her lungs at the soft but heated caress.

"We...shouldn't do this," she murmured her token protest as he lifted his head.

"You're right."

They stared at each other, waiting for the other to stand up and make the first move back to respectability and normalcy. But he didn't move. And she couldn't move. The second time he kissed her was just as hot as before, but there was nothing soft about it. It was a claiming kiss, designed to mark her down to the soul. She kissed back with everything she had, throwing herself into the wrongness of the situation and getting caught up in a whirlpool of desire. The more she reminded herself of how bad it was, the faster the whirlpool spun, and the harder it sucked her down to its depths where she couldn't lift a single finger to save herself. She was drowning in the inky depths and she didn't care.

By mutual, silent consent, they cleared the kitchen table and then met with another hard, passionate kiss. Her nipples were tight and perky beneath her silky nightgown. He pushed the robe from her shoulders, letting the material swish to the floor so he could get to her full breasts. He cupped them both, squeezing gently in rhythm with his mouth, his thumbs brushing over the peaks until they were harder than ever. He kissed down her throat and closed his mouth around one of the nipples, sucking on her through the material of her nightgown. When he lifted his head, there was a big wet spot on the gown, and he did the same to the other side, grinding his teeth down on the flesh, sending a million sparks to her clit, which fluttered and jerked in response to everything he was doing with his mouth.

He lifted her by the waist and she wrapped her long, bare legs around him, allowing him to lift her to the kitchen table. His hard cock peeked out from his boxers, and all she had to do was push the flap aside with her knuckles. Her pussy clenched at the sight of his dick, at the feel of it against her thigh and under her palm. She couldn't remember the last time she wrapped her hand around a shaft that was so thick, or opened her legs for a cock so long. She was opening her legs for him now, pushing her ass closer to the edge of the table. He hiked her gown up higher around her hips and pulled her panties to the side, revealing just how aroused she was. He ran his fingertips up and down her slit, dipping between the swollen lips to find her clit. He pressed on the nub of flesh and she shuddered, arching her spine as her entire body contracted with pleasure.

"Sorry it's not more fancy," he murmured against her mouth, stealing the words between long, desperate kisses. "But it's been a very long time for me."

"I don't need fancy."

"I don't have a condom. I'm safe though, got one hundred percent on my last physical."

"I'm on the pill. It's fine."

He breathed a sigh of relief. "Good, because I can't see myself stopping now."

She shook her head. "No, don't stop. Please don't stop. Oh...yes..." She felt the blunt tip nudging at her tight opening and then the tip was inside and it occurred to her that this really was the very last second. She could still stop them before they both crossed a line they didn't want to cross. Instead, she flexed her legs and pulled him closer, drawing him even deeper inside until he was fully sheathed. Now each kiss was one of necessity, the only way to muffle their mutual moans of pleasure and need.

"Fuck me," she whispered. "Hard. Fuck me hard." She wanted to feel and know the strength of his beautifully cut and conditioned body. He was a Marine, even if he hadn't been with a woman in a long time, and she wanted to know just how deep his training went. He lifted her ass off the table, pulling her even closer, locking their bodies as tightly as possible. He spun around, pushed her up against the counter, and began to move his hips. Too slow at first. Slow and maddening. She balled her hands into fists and hit the firm, ungiving muscles of his back.

"Impatient," he whispered.

"I don't have the time for patience," she countered, pleased to squeeze out so many words on her half-breath. His cock felt amazing inside of her, and she couldn't stop herself from clenching down around him, squeezing him tight, holding him in place.

"You don't want me to really fuck you."

"Uh, yeah, I do."

"Okay, but I'll warn you, most people don't walk away from that experience unchanged."

"What does that mean?"

"If I fuck you like you want, you'll turn into my little cockslut. I'm perfectly fine with that, but you might not be."

"I'm willing to risk it."

He smiled. "You're the boss, boss."

Within seconds, she understood exactly what he meant. She did believe that size wasn't the most important factor. A man with a horse cock who didn't know how to use it—or couldn't last for more than a few minutes—was no good to her. Phil wasn't exactly huge, but he was clever and had a ton of stamina. She didn't know if Jeff was clever, but he had pure, physical, raw power. He pounded into her with harsh grunts, beads of sweat popping up on his brow as he worked his hips. She rode his cock for all she was worth, pulling away from his mouth and closing her teeth down on the muscle in his shoulder to order to keep quiet. She wanted to shout down the entire house. She wanted to scream his name and beg him and plead to God to not let this end. All the reasons she shouldn't have his cock paled in comparison to the unrelenting, perfect pounding, the divine pleasure of their coupling. She didn't even think about how easy it would be to get caught in a house full of people, all of whom know damned well there's leftover pie in the kitchen.

But by some miracle, they're not interrupted. Jeff carried her back to the table, laying her on her back and holding her legs straight up in the air. At this angle, it's easier to hit her back wall, it's easier to saw against her G-spot and carry her to even greater heights. She grabs whatever she can reach, lodging a napkin between her teeth to stop the new wave of screams building in her throat. She can't get enough of the sight of him and doesn't close her eyes once while he pistons his hips.

She felt it building at the base of her

spine and behind her knees and in the trembling muscles of her thighs. Her stomach clenched, and she was close...close...climbing higher and getting closer to the inevitability of it. She knows he's going to cum inside of her, and she thinks about returning to her husband with his brother's jizz drying on her thighs, and even though the thought should have been enough to shock her with guilt, she only bears down on Jeff's cock, fucking back every time he slammed forward. The pleasure crystalized then, intensified to something she couldn't even say she experienced before. His hand came down on her mouth, blocking whatever sound the make-shift gag couldn't get, and she couldn't get enough air, but she didn't care. They rocked and jerked together, his cock spasming as she fluttered around him and when everything ultimately shattered, they were clinging to each other, sweat mingling, and bodies in perfect unity.

9 ADULT FUN

Natasha and Jeremy had once been very sexually adventurous, but now, they have a son and a normal life, and they've put that behind them. Mostly, every once in awhile, they meet a man who neither can refuse—who neither want to refuse! Kurt, aka Thor, is one of those fine specimens. Natasha and Jeremy work so well together because they always share the same goal, and the big beautiful Nordic man doesn't have any idea what's about to hit him.

Jeremy knew the big man's name, but he always thought of him as Thor, which was far more fitting than the name his parents had saddled him with at birth— Kurt. He was six and a half feet of solid, thick muscle, with a thick blond beard and long, flowing blond hair. The first time Jeremy saw him, he had about six kids hanging off his massive arms, each one of them laughing with delight as he lifted them from the ground. They dangled from him like they weighed nothing, and his laughter was just as delighted as theirs. He was a regular at the park, a single father who brought his daughter to play every weekend. At first, the rest of the parents had been skeptical of the giant walking in their midst, and more than a little nervous when he lumbered towards their children, who seemed even more miniature when they stood next to him. But it didn't take long for everybody to figure out that he wasn't just harmless, he was the sweetest person who ever lived. Jeremy found himself going to the park more often with his wife, Natasha, who was now making it a point to go every weekend, probably for the exact same reason.

Her motivations became clearer when she walked over there on days that their son, Brent, was at his grandmother's house. Jeremy wasn't jealous. Far from it. It had been years since anybody caught Natasha's attention, and since he could only indulge in the other half of his desires when she was on board, he was more than eager for her to approach Thor. That was how it always worked. She made the first move, tested the waters, and lured the prey into a trap with her big green eyes and her perfectly curved body. Most of the time that was more than enough to catch a guy and keep him, even after he realized that she was a package deal.

It was difficult to get a read on Thor, though. He was gregarious and boisterous, and he already considered Natasha a friend. Hell, he considered everybody at the park a friend and had already escalated to greeting her—and Jeremy— with huge bear hugs that left no doubt of just how strong and big he was. Jeremy couldn't help but notice the monster he was packing in his trousers. He announced he would be more than happy to join Natasha and her husband for dinner at their house the next night when his daughter was with her mother. Jeremy could barely keep his excitement to himself, most of his day completely lost to thoughts of getting Thor's magnificent body stripped naked. He had the uneasy feeling that Natasha could read his mind because every time their eyes met, her lips twitched in a knowing smile.

Thor dominated their home from the second he walked into the door, the apartment suddenly seeming tiny, toy-like. He could have stopped everything they owned down to splinters and dust. He brought a giant bottle of wine and pulled

Jeremy into a bone crushing hug as he walked in the door. "It is great to see you, my friend!"

"It's good to see you, too..." Jeremy sought his memory for the right name. "Kurt."

"I have brought wine. Where should I put it?"

"I'll take that," Natasha said as she floated out of the kitchen. "Thank you, that was very thoughtful of you."

"It was my pleasure."

"Why don't you and Jeremy have a seat? Dinner will be done soon." She smiled at Thor and dropped a small wink Jeremy's direction before disappearing back through the kitchen door.

"You have a lovely home!"

"Thank you. Have a seat."

Thor dropped his weight down to the couch and sprawled back, his arms draped over the back of the couch, his legs spread in front of him. He essentially took up the whole sofa, but Jeremy was happy to take the chair opposite of him. Maybe if he studied him long enough, he'd start to make some sort of sense. How could anybody be so big? How could a man be so...pretty?

"Thank you for inviting me. It has been a long time since I've enjoyed the company of friends."

"Really? Been busy?"

"No, but I do not have many friends."

Jeremy was quite surprised to hear that. Yes, his interest in the giant was less than pure, but he was a good guy with a big heart. Why wouldn't he have dozens of friends? No reason that Jeremy could see.

"Well, you're always welcome here. We like your company."

Thor's smile was at least a thousand watts. "Thank you, my friend, I enjoy your company as well."

Dinner was delicious, of course. Thor did most of the talking, bragging about his daughter, and recounting stories from his time as the Strong Man in a traveling carnival. Jeremy found himself laughing along more than he expected. Thor was a great storyteller with a fine sense of humor. Just more reason to like him, and Jeremy was already worried about liking him too much. But would Thor feel the same way about him? Could he? He and Natasha both agreed that she would have to make the first move because he was less likely to punch her if she suggested something he didn't like. Not that Jeremy really thought Thor would punch him. He seemed to be more than aware of his strength, and he didn't have a malicious bone in his body.

After dinner, Thor sprawled on the couch again, but this time, Natasha joined him. She sat close enough to touch him, and Jeremy saw that Thor definitely noticed. He kept glancing between Natasha and Jeremy with a confused furrow of his brow. When her hand went to his thigh, the furrow deepened.

"Do you have a girlfriend, Kurt?"

"No. I do not have time for any relationships, sadly. Most women do not understand that my daughter comes first in my life. Or they aren't willing to actually accept that."

Natasha frowned sympathetically. "That sounds like it must be very lonely."

"It can be," Thor admitted. "I would not wish it on anybody. But I love my daughter very much, and she brings a great deal of joy to my life."

"We know exactly what you mean. We weren't even sure we wanted kids when Brent came along, but we never regretted it for a second."

"He's a good boy. He always treats Ellie with respect. He will grow up to be a fine, strong man."

Jeremy smiled despite himself. He didn't need anybody to tell him he had a good kid, but something about Thor's praise was so direct and sincere that it warmed him.

"But sometimes...it's good to be without the kids, too. Remember what it's like to be adults." Her hand moved a little further up her thigh, and Thor stiffened, the languid grace suddenly gone from his limbs.

"Mrs. Johnson?"

"Don't be nervous, Kurt. My husband and I...we want to help with your loneliness."

"You two wish to have sex with me?"

"Yes," Natasha said, looking him in the eye.

He looked to Jeremy. "You do not have a problem with me fucking your wife?" He tilted his head. "Or do wish for me to fuck you?"

"Um...well, both if you're okay with that."

Thor continued to study him, his eyes slowly traveling up and down Jeremy's body. "Very well. I accept your offer. We should move this to the bedroom."

Jeremy and Natasha shared a surprise glance that quickly turned into mutual smiles. Yes, moving it to the bedroom was definitely a good idea.

Turns out, kids weren't the only ones who enjoyed climbing all over Thor's massive frame. Jeremy had never been picked up in his adult life, but Thor whisked him off the floor with an arm around his waist, Natasha fitting snugly in the crook of his other arm. He carried them both to the bedroom, gently depositing them on the bed before stripping his clothes off without a hint of shame. Natasha's mouth fell open. That was fine. Jeremy's was watering, and he probably was about five seconds away from straight-up drooling.

"Thank you for inviting me to your bed. It has been quite a while for me."

Natasha took him by the hand and pulled him down to the mattress, immediately swinging her leg over his hips to straddle him. Jeremy busied himself with shucking his clothes and peeling hers from her body while she sampled every inch of Thor's skin that she could reach. Thor dropped his head back, his chin pointed to the ceiling, his eyes closed with a look of pure bliss as Natasha took her time licking and kissing and nibbling down his throat and chest. Her mouth was hot and perfect, and Jeremy knew exactly how good it felt, how adept she was at starting a million fires beneath his skin until he was burning to be inside her.

Once all three of them were completely naked, Jeremy joined them on the bed, kneeling between Thor's legs. His hard cock jutted from between a thick thatch of blonde curls, the shaft pressed to his wife's ass. Jeremy dropped to his hands and knees and rubbed his face against the velvety smooth skin of his shaft. He glided his lips from the tip to the base, licked over his throbbing vein on the journey back to the crown, licking past the salty-bitter taste of his sweat to the cleaner, purer skin. Jeremy's cock stiffened to his full length, though that was considerably less than Thor's. He didn't have the time or the energy to be jealous, though. Why be jealous over what was clearly a natural treasure?

Jeremy fumbled for the strip of condoms in his nightstand drawer, tossing the whole lot of them on the mattress within reach. He had the feeling they'd only just be enough—he and Natasha were compatible in many ways, including their insatiable appetites. They'd ride Thor as long as his mighty hammer could take it. He kissed a trail up Natasha's spine, gliding his mouth up her body until he reached her ear, and she was leaning back against his chest.

"Will you get his dick good and wet for me, sweetheart?"

"I'd love to."

"Will you get me good and wet for him?"

"Of course."

He unrolled a condom down Thor's shaft, and even though he bought magnums for this night, the condom barely made it half way down his shaft. Good God. For the first time he wondered if his eyes were bigger than his stomach—so to speak. Just because he wanted to sink down on that thick pole didn't mean he would be able to. When Thor was ready, Natasha sat up, repositioning her pussy over the thick head. Jeremy put a hand on her hip and guided her back and down, watching, entranced, as Thor's huge dick disappeared an inch at a time, his wife's pussy swallowing it up. The only sound was her sharp gasps as she stretched around him, but by the time she was fully seated, those gasps were a series of loud, breathy moans.

"Ride him," Jeremy whispered in her ear before pushing himself to his feet. He repositioned himself, standing over Thor, his ass level with Natasha's face. She knew what to do, didn't hesitate to spread his cheeks and thrust her tongue forward, penetrating him with familiar gusto. She wiggled her velvet tongue around his opening, awakening nerve endings that had been asleep too long.

Thor moaned, and the mattress shifted precariously beneath Jeremy's feet. He bent his knees, popping his ass back, grinding against her greedy mouth. He looked over his shoulder, watching as she rocked on him, keeping him buried all the way in her pussy as she shifted back and forth. When he glanced back to Thor, he saw the big man's eyes were open and locked on Jeremy's cock. Jeremy wasn't even touching himself, just letting his hard length bob freely, and jerking every time she thrust. Both of Thor's hands were free, so Jeremy took him by the wrist and guided it to his cock, moaning when the huge, strong fingers closed around him as tightly as a vice. He loved the way Natasha touched him, but there were some things he still craved that she couldn't give him.

Thor stroked him with hard, slow strokes, pumping his fist and squeezing and making Jeremy throb everywhere, from the tip of his cock to the back of his eyes. Natasha was moaning, too, her lips vibrating against his flesh, the sound traveling through him directly to his dick. He had to look over his shoulder again, though with her face buried in his ass; he couldn't see anything except the exquisite line of her spine down to the perfectly rounded curve of her ass. She was moving faster and faster, and that's why she always got to go first. Just watching her go crazy on a cock made him hot, he didn't care who she was riding as long as she was breaking him, taking what she wanted and everything else he had to offer.

Thor's eyes were glazed over with pleasure, his muscles flexing with every stroke and thrust. He was like a work of art, a statue—or maybe a God—come to life. There was undeniable grace in his body, but more than that, Jeremy could see how closely he checked himself. He was letting Natasha have her way with him, and though his grip was firm, Jeremy knew he wasn't using a fraction of a percentage of his actual strength. What would it be like to break the big guy's control? Would it be fun? Would he regret it? Too many times in Jeremy's life the answer of one came hand in hand with the answer to the other. The things he always enjoyed the most carried some level of regret, even if that was bruises that wouldn't fade away for weeks.

Natasha's moans grew louder, came faster. She was moving in different ways now, too, rocking further forward, slamming back harder. She found the angle she liked, and Jeremy's cock leaked copious amounts of pre-come as he listened to her, moved with her, pumped his hips against Thor's massive palm. Her fingers dug into his flesh, her nails sinking deeper and deeper as the tension increased. She lost control of her mouth. Her tongue was still moving, but it wasn't with the same steady beat or precision as before. Her face disappeared, her hand traveling up his body, scratching over his ass before he felt the fingertips pressing against his entrance. She pushed two digits in without warning, her hand moving in rhythm with her hips. Jeremy's mouth fell open, but he couldn't gasp for breath, couldn't inhale or exhale as the burn from her fingers ignited a spark in his stomach. The fire burned through him, made him flushed with need, and then she was shouting. Incoherently, frantically, her voice rising and falling with the waves of pleasure. He knew her sounds well, knew that he could track every orgasm as it broke through her.

Thor's facade broke, the intent look on his face giving way to something very much like shock. His face froze that way, and Jeremy knew exactly what he was feeling. There was unbelievable power in Natasha's body, and nothing unleashed it like the force of her pleasure, each climax spreading the sparks that would ignite into more pleasure. She wasn't going to stop on her own. Did Thor realize that? She'd keep going until he pushed her off or his dick was soft—she could be a real greedy bitch when she really got going. Jeremy loved that about her.

"Your turn," she gasped out long before he expected her to.

"Are you sure?"

"Yes," she moaned, though she indulged in a few more slow strokes before dismounting. He waited until she was stretched out beside them to lower himself to his knees, sliding back until he felt the slick head against his ass. He was so wet from Natasha's pussy and her copious cum that Jeremy had absolutely no problem sinking back, taking him in, and expanding to accommodate his impressive girth. There was only a hint of pain. Mostly, it was a slow burn, a heady pressure, the sense that he was being completely split open. His eyes rolled back in his head, and he surrendered completely to the pleasure. Thor's hand went to his hip, the other one still stroking his cock, and oh he was going to have to stop doing that. Jeremy couldn't handle the combination, it felt too fucking good.

Natasha watched Thor's hand for a moment, watched the way Jeremy's head disappeared and reappeared from sight, her tongue gliding over her shining lips. He tried to tell her to stop, tried to shake his head, but either he failed to convey the message or she was happy to ignore him. Her hot mouth touching his tender crown was the final spark he needed, and her lips were barely wrapped around his cock before he erupted, shooting his full load in her mouth. She swallowed it, sucking more from his slit, coaxing as much of the salty fluid from him as she could.

"Have you had enough?" Thor's question rumbled through his chest.

Jeremy shook his head. "Not until you do, big guy."

Thor's smile was wide, and suddenly, the ceiling traded places with the floor and everything was topsy-turvy. Jeremy stared up from his new position on the back, too stunned to make a single sound. Not that he would protest, even if he could find the strength to speak. Thor's cock was now driving into him at an almost inhuman pace, each thrust hitting directly against his prostate. He knew men could have multiple orgasms, but he'd never experienced them himself. Not until Thor hit that most sensitive spot and fireworks went off, his cock jerking out clear fluid as his brain short-circuited and he lost control of his limbs. He thrashed helplessly as a child until Thor caught him by the biceps and rested his weight there, effectively pinning him in place, pounding him harder than before.

"Oh this is what it looks like when he breaks. Oh shit! this is good...fun...not bad at all...nothing bad here..."

Jeremy's only warning that the crazy ride was about to stop was Thor's sudden roar. He reared back, looking not unlike a lion, and his cock jerked so hard in Jeremy's ass that he was pretty sure it triggered another orgasm. He wasn't entirely sure because he blacked out for a few seconds, and when he came to again, Thor was lying on his back like a big, satisfied bear, and Natasha was curled like a sweet kitten between their sweaty, heaving bodies.

"That was great fun!"

"Yes," Jeremy and Natasha breathed at the same time. Jeremy was going to be so fucking sore the next day—but he was counting on that. It'd make it all the better when Natasha bent him over and pegged him like her little bitch. Great fun, indeed.

10 THE BLACK RIDER

Jamie is a cowboy without a place to go or a dollar to his name. There's a job opening at the Rocking J Ranch, and there's just one thing standing in his way, the lone rider he spots on the plains, riding hell for leather towards the ranch. Intrigued, he follows. When he realizes his mysterious black rider is a woman, he's more than intrigued. He's hard as a rock and willing to do anything she orders.

Jamie saw the black rider at a distance, hunched over the Indian pony and riding hard for the ranch. The rider took a diagonal route that met very closely with his own path, and that's when he noticed the long, black tresses flowing out behind her like a cape. More than intrigued enough to forget all about good sense, he spurred his horse into a faster run, cutting to the right to join her path. Her little mustang was fast, bred for speed over the flat plains, and Jamie didn't expect to catch up with her, but he didn't want to lose sight of her, either. He pushed his tired horse harder than he should have; his curiosity only heightened when he realized they already shared a destination. The Rocking J Ranch, established two decades earlier by Joseph Johnson, the first ranch in the territory, and as a result, Joseph Johnson was the most powerful man within two hundred miles.

Jamie knew this. But somehow, he didn't make the connection between the powerful cattle baron and the mysterious woman riding hell for leather through the high grass. He didn't even draw the obvious conclusion when she ran her pony right into the barn. By the time he entered the building, she had already dismounted, pulling the bonnet from her head and allowing her black hair to tumble down her back. She was alone with her horse, and he realized she wasn't wearing a dress under her long black coat—she wore pants, like a man. She also didn't ride side-saddle, and that seemed to be confirmation enough that she held some employ in the house. A maid, or a governess; something that would give her a bit more freedom to behave a little less ladylike.

Jamie didn't really care about the explanation. All he knew was that he liked her. He didn't need to know her name or anything else about her. He saw the way she sat on a horse and knew how well she could ride—that literally told Jamie everything he needed to know about her. He swung his left leg over the horse and dropped to the ground, the sound of his boots hitting the hard dirt startling her into turning around. When she did, he lost his breath, his chest heaved with shock at the sight of her perfect face. It was true that the woemn were few and far between on the cattle trail, but she was still the most beautiful woman he'd ever laid eyes on. Her blue eyes captivated him, and her high cheekbones and full lips entranced him. He longed to touch her skin, wanted to smell the wind and the sunshine in her hair.

"Who are you?" she snapped.

"Jamie, ma'am." He bowed like it was the most natural thing in the world. Jamie was pretty sure he'd never bowed to anybody before in his life. "Your servant."

"My servant?" she snorted and turned back to her horse, loosening the saddle straps. "I don't need anybody's help."

"Of course not. May I ask you a favor?"

"If you must."

"Could you grant me your name?"

She snorted again. "My oh my, you nearly sound genteel. Most of these brutes didn't even have mothers, much less a proper introduction to manners."

"I'm not like most brutes, miss."

"Clearly not. Here, take this." She passed the saddle over to him and nodded at the rack where the saddles were stored. He found the empty spot for the tack, barely resisting the impulse to press his nose to the shiny leather and inhale deeply.

"So, about that favor?" Jamie asked, turning back to her.

"Ah, yes. I'm Melanie. It's a pleasure to meet you, Jamie."

"The pleasure is mine," Jamie said, taking her offered hand and bringing it up to his mouth. He pressed his lips to her knuckles and raised his gaze to meet hers. Her skin was rough, wind-chapped, and she smelled like sunshine and leather. His nostrils quivered as he inhaled the scent of her in and held it deeply in his lungs. Behind her, the horse stamped impatiently, and she pulled her fingers free of his grip to see to the animal.

"I take it you've come looking for a job. Sorry to tell you, but you're a little late."

"I know. I'm not a trail hand."

"What do you do?"

"Personal security. Stick close to me

and I'll make sure no harm comes to you."

"Somehow I find that far from comforting Mr..."

"Just Jamie, miss. And you should find it comforting. I'm one of the sharpest shooters in the west."

"Is that a fact?"

"Yes, ma'am."

"Then why aren't you in any of the penny novels?"

"Well I've only killed three men. You need to kill at least six before you get a book."

"I wasn't aware of that."

"Oh, yeah, it's the rule of thumb back east. Anything less than six just bores them to death."

"But you already have three? It sounds like trouble might follow you. Why would I want that hanging around?"

"Oh, I assure you, miss, trouble doesn't follow me. But I find it when there's something to be found. You never know what lurks in the hearts of men. But sometimes, I can suss it out."

"Sounds like a remarkable talent."

"It's saved a few lives." Jamie smiled and handed her the currying comb. She ran it over her pony's neck, collecting the loose hair and dirt from his coat. "Now, all I'm asking for is the chance to protect yours."

"That's where things might go poorly for

you. I don't need anybody to protect me." Jamie didn't see where the gun came from. One second, she held nothing but the comb, and in the next second, the grooming tool was gone and a six-shooter was in its place. Pointed directly at his heart. Jamie immediately put his hands up and smiled, flashing every bit of charm he possessed.

"Clearly. And I apologize for my error in judgment."

Instead of putting the gun away, she took a step closer to him. He stood his ground, his body expanding with the very sight of her. She was truly remarkable, a dream come to life, stunning from head to toe. He didn't know if she planned to shoot him, and that just made her all the more alluring. He had her name, but he had no idea who she was, and there were a million possibilities between them. His death was among them. Somehow, he was completely at ease with that.

"Do you have any sense of self-preservation?" she asked.

"I like to think I do," he replied.

"So you'll do whatever it takes to stay alive?" A slight smile played in the corners of her full lips.

"Been in plenty of tight corners. Already proved that more than once."

"We'll see. Get on your knees," she commanded.

Jamie didn't know if he was about to be robbed, executed, or worse. But he still hit his knees, as she instructed, and looked up at her with a silent question—what else would you have me do? He knew he was being a slave to his dick, and nine times out of ten...hell who was he kidding? Ten times out of ten, that was a very bad idea. But if she was his last very bad idea, he'd count that as a clear victory and consider himself a winner as he rode into the next life.

She lifted her arm and brought the tail of her coat around, letting it enclose him in darkness. She brought the other side around, leaving only his legs and boots visible. He put his hands up, encircling her waist and struggling to catch his breath. It was hot under the coat, and his nose was full of the scent of a hard ride: leather and wind and horse sweat.

"You know what to do, don't you?" Melanie asked, looking down at the silhouette of him shrouded in her coat.

He thought he did. He hoped he did. Because there really was only one thing for him to do, and if she had a different idea, she'd probably shoot him right there and then. There was a certain wariness as he reached up to unbuckle her belt and tug at the buttons holding her fly together. As he pulled the pants down her thighs, revealing the sweet mound between her legs, he had to admit there were some advantages to pants over the more complicated layers of skirts. He pressed his face between her thighs, nuzzling his nose against her hair and finally catching the smell of her, untainted by anything else. There was only her musk and her sweat and her heady arousal. He shoved her pants down to her knees and then cupped her pussy, gently pulling her lips apart. Her nub peaked out from the petals of flesh, and he stuck his tongue out experimentally. The tip of his pink flesh touched hers, and she immediately gripped the back of his head and pushed her hips forward, grinding herself against his mouth.

He occasionally paid for the taste of cunny, but generally, he was more focused on getting his dick wet. Especially since the bar women and prostitutes usually were so high on opium and numb that they couldn't even feel what he was doing with his tongue. Melanie wasn't like them, though. She could feel every second of it, and her body was in constant motion, responding to every curious flick of his tongue. He dragged it over her lips, tasting every bit of her before focusing on her nub once again. That was clearly her favorite spot, and the more pressure he used, the more he was rewarded, both with her sounds of pleasure and with the sweet taste of her arousal, flowing from inside of her to coat his face and paint his tongue.

She used her grip to keep his face pressed to her pussy, and there was no denying her strength. The same strength she used to keep her headstrong mustang in line she used on Jamie, guiding his mouth, showing him exactly where she wanted to feel him, exactly how he should be moving over her swollen, sensitive flesh. His cock throbbed, and he wanted to be buried in this woman. He wanted to take her with a hard, demanding thrust. He wanted to fill her with one firm stroke and then ride her for the rest of the night. Or lie back and let her ride him, whipping his thighs like he was her steed, screaming at him to go faster and faster, to race her to the sky.

"Faster," she moaned, as if she could read his thoughts. "That's it. Oh, that's it..."

Then her hips started to move, taking over everything. She rotated them, grinding harder and harder against his mouth. He sucked her flesh between his lips, flicking his tongue over the sensitive tip. She lost control then, her hips bucking hard, slamming forward. He had to grip her by the hips and hold her in place, though she fought him. She fought him harder than any untrained, headstrong filly he'd ever touched. Somehow, though, the fight only made it better, and more of her sweet juices coated her and spread across his face. He tried to lap up as much as he could, but somehow, there was always more than he could lick away.

Clearly, she was somewhat experienced and not completely innocent, but had anybody ever entered her? There was one easy way to tell. All he had to do was slide his hand down her thigh and let his long finger slide against her slit. He touched her gently, but even the light pressure was enough to set her off, her breath coming in faster, higher gasps. That definitely didn't sound like a stop. At least, not to his ears. He teased her opening a little bit longer, tracing around the soft skin, and he was sure there was never anything softer in the world. She bucked her hips and whimpered, widening her stance even further, giving him all the encouragement he needed to continue. He slipped into her wet, welcoming heat, sighing as the oh-so-tight channel clenched around him. There was no barrier stopping his finger, but that didn't mean she'd ever had another man. She was certainly tight enough to be a virgin.

He curved the finger inside of her,

making a beckoning gesture, as though urging somebody closer to him. She cried out as he caressed places that he was sure had never been touched before. One more time and he sensed a change in her, a sudden tightening in her thighs and her stomach. The smell of her juices was stronger than ever, and all it took was one more tiny wiggle of his finger to send her over the edge. Both hands went to the back of his head, and she keened through her bone-rattling pleasure; her entire body shaking against Jamie's face. He kept attacking her with his tongue, not giving her a single second to catch her breath. He knew there was more where this came from, knew he could coax her to the top of another peak and then drown in her juices as she sailed over the edge.

At first, she tried to push him away, panting that it was enough, that she was too sensitive, and that she had enough. Then switching tactics, warning him that they wouldn't be alone for very long, that her father could walk in at any second and catch them. Jamie didn't care. He was already prepared to lay his life down for this woman, and if he did cross over to the other side, he wanted to leave her with plenty of good memories.

It only took a few moments before she stopped pushing him away. Seconds later, she was pulling him against her, and he knew they were off to the races again. He pumped his wrist, adding a second finger, working his digits in and out of her slowly.

"Faster," she whispered between moans. "Please...I need...I need more..."

"Yes, yes, yes," Jamie said against her throbbing nub. "What more do you need? Tell me."

"I need..."

"Say it."

"I want you...I want you inside of me...oh I need it."

Jamie jumped to his feet, ripping his pants open as he straightened. He wrapped one arm around her, and she finished kicking her pants off, jumping to wrap her legs around his waist. He pushed her back up against the wall, his rigid cock seeking her heat. He dragged his crown up and down her lips before settling at her opening. She pushed her hips down, encompassing him in her slick warmth, and Jamie felt like he'd finally come home. She moved like he expected her to, all controlled passion and heated dominance. He never touched a woman who knew what she wanted and took it with such ease. This must have been what her mustang felt like, simultaneously under her complete control and yet totally free. His heart pounded triumphantly, his blood roared through his body, and he thought his feet might be leaving the ground next.

Their bodies pulsed together, surged together, moved in a perfect, primal rhythm. He sought out her mouth. At first, she turned away from him, from her own scent and taste, but he caught her by the chin and held her in place, invading her mouth with his tongue. She couldn't resist him, couldn't turn away from him, and he plunge into her silky softness again and again, taking her with his mouth and his cock.

She started to clench, started to pull tight and tremble, and he recognized the signs. He didn't want her to be so close. She was going to drive him right over the edge, and he didn't want this to end. He knew this was as fleeting as a sunset, perfect and golden and over all too soon, never to be experienced again. No matter how many more he witnessed in his lifetime, they never lasted long enough. Like this would end all too soon.

She yanked his head back, pulling her mouth away long enough to pant for breath. There was an edge to her breathing—a certain sound that grew and grew until she was quaking with it. Her pussy gripped his dick so tight he couldn't hold himself back, and he exploded deep inside of her, his cock jerking, his balls pulling close to his body as he filled her with his seed.

"My father..."

"What about your father?" Jamie murmured.

"If you want a job here, he better not let you catch him corrupting his daughter." She unwrapped her legs from him and touched down to the ground, letting his soft member slip from her.

"Does that mean I can't corrupt her again?"

"It means you best watch yourself. You never know who might be watching, Cowboy."

She pulled her pants up and adjusted her coat, leaving him to stare after her like the love-wounded fool he was.

AUTHOR'S NOTE

Readers: I want to expand a few of the stories to see where the characters can be explored further. If there are any of the stories that you would like to read more about again, I'd love to hear from you!

Visit my blog at www.kelliegranier.com

Join my newsletter for free exclusive previews
www.kelliegranier.com/in

Follow me on Twitter at
www.twitter.com/kelliegranier

Like my page on Facebook at
www.facebook.com/kelliegranier

Discover my books at major ebook retailers everywhere.